The Treasure of the Crystal Cave

~A Fairy Tale Fantasy~

Kelsie R. Gates

Primix Publishing
485c US Highway 1 South
Suite 100
Iselin, NJ 08830
www.primixpublishing.com
Phone: 1-800-538-5788

Published by Primix Publishing: 09/18/2024

ISBN: 979-8-89194-292-9(sc)
ISBN: 979-8-89194-293-6(e)

Library of Congress Control Number: 2024916425

Contents

Chapter 1 – the arrival - a key 1

Chapter 2 – a Friend - Love 7

Chapter 3 – journeys - a Beggar - Treasure 13
                              Alaric's ... story 13

Chapter 4 – Tagg..21

Chapter 5 – an Angry Earth 29

Chapter 6 – the White Wolf - a River to Cross.....35

Chapter 7 – an Old Man 41

Chapter 8 – the Crystal Cave..................................47

Chapter 9 – escape From Crystal Cave 51

Chapter 10 – the Sisters 57

Chapter 11 – the Wolf - my Brother.......................67

Chapter 12 – a tiny Gold Key - a big Black Raven 75

Chapter 13 – no Grand Plan 81

Chapter 14 – an Ice River - Pursuit 87

Chapter 15 – - the key to Freedom - 95

Chapter 16 – - out from the Dark - 101
Chapter 17 – - confrontation -......................105
Chapter 18 – - decisions - 113
Chapter 19 – - a bad Dream - 119
Chapter 20 – - transformation -....................123
Chapter 21 – - the Coronation - the Crown - 129
Chapter 22 – - two Weddings - 135
Chapter 23 – - lightning Bolts - a pink Cloud - .141

■ ■ ■ ■ ■ ■ ■ ■ ■ ■

One will come.
To save country and kingdom
Blown out of a dark nights wind
Down to earth like an angel
On wings of white gossamer
Having the sweet innocence of a child
Fearing nothing and no one

■ ■ ■ ■ ■ ■ ■ ■ ■ ■

Another book by Kelsie R. Gates

Chad'tu

This book was written
In memory of

Linda Fong

~ And for all that cared ~

Chapter 1

the arrival ~ a key

Through the fury of the dark night and howling wind she fell. Lightning filled the sky with bright flashes of its anger. Like a banshee, the wind whipped about her, grabbing with its cold wet fingers, at her hair and flapping gown. It ripped at her as she tumbled toward Mother Earth.

She franticly caught her breath. For a moment, she searched her mind for the correct words, which would slow her fall. Gasping for breath, she screamed out the words. Instantly, no longer than a heartbeat, two beautiful white glistening wings, sprouted from her back.

With a strong flap of wings, her descent slowed. She landed softly on the damp grass of a meadow surrounded by huge tall trees. She pulled her long black hair back from her face. Her dark eyes flashing, she surveyed her surroundings. Miiliinda looked like an angel, dressed as she was, in a shimmering silver and white silk gown, its edges trimmed in gold. Although beautiful, she could well take care of herself, for she had been trained by a mage in the arts of mystical magic

That was easy she thought. Having only recently acquired her magical powers, which sometimes worked, and other times didn't, due to the wrong words spoken, she was sure. At the open end of the meadow were granite boulders of every size and shape strewn across the ground, as if a giant hand had tossed them there.

In all of her sixteen years, never had she seen such a forest as this.

Living in Chinnder, she had never seen trees that were as tall as the ones that surrounded the meadow. She stared up at them in the murky gloom of darkness, barely able to see their tops. They must be at least three hundred feet tall and as big around as the Quark where she had been born. Between the giant trees were many smaller trees, their branches reaching up and out. Reaching for what? They looked like small children reaching up to be held by loving arms. She guessed they must be the offspring of the giant trees.

Looking about the strange forest, she laughed nervously into the dark night. "Ha! Ha! Ha! My name is Miiliinda and I have magical powers, so do not dare fool with me." She finished with a forced smile, wondering where she could possible be.

She gathered up several soft damp twigs along with tuffs of grass. With a few spoken words of magic, the dampness disappeared. Then another ancient word was spoken. The twigs and grass became alive and interwove, forming a bed of sorts, a place upon which she could rest.

Tired, she stretched and lay down on the bed made of thick grass. Pulling her long black hair close around her for warmth, she laid her head upon the grass-covered twigs and closing her black almond shaped eyes fell fast asleep.

She slept lightly. Even though asleep, her subconscious mind reached out searching the edges of the forbidding forest. Sometime later, she awoke with a start. Something had gently touched her mind. Sensing a presence at the edge of the woods, she pretended to still sleep, her eyes closed. Not reacting and focusing all her senses, her mind probed instantly toward the place from which it emanated,

Without moving, she opened one eye slowly, peered at the dark quiet forest. Nothing moved. No wind rustled through the branches, no night birds sang, just deathly quiet. Still, something had awakened her. Taking a second, she wondered what to do? *Mother always said, face your fears.*

Faster than the blink of an eye, she sprang to her feet, spun quickly three times. Looking about she stopped, pointed a finger into the foreboding darkness and yelled, "I know you are there." Unable to penetrate the darkness she paused, catching her breath, she glanced apprehensively to the left and right. "Who are you?" she said in the bravest voice she could muster.

Unaware she was clenching her gown, she waited for a response. Again, only silence answered her question. Losing some of her fear, she took a small step forward and stopped. Raising a small fist, she yelled at the forest once again. "I'm not afraid of you, I'm not afraid of anything on this earth. I am Miiliinda, and... and I have many powers, so step forth, before I get really angry." Still, nothing moved.

From the corner of an eye, she caught a flash of movement, just inside the forest edge. Quickly she turned and glimpsed something white, moving at great speed among the trees, really just a blur of white it moved so fast. Then it was gone. *Did I see something, or was it my mind playing tricks.*

If something is out there, I will create an invisible shield, to protect me, And, with a few magic words, she did. *This magic shield will protect me against everything.* With that thought, she pulled her gown tightly around her for warmth and lying back on the makeshift bed feeling safe from all things, she fell fast asleep.

The next morning she stood, stretched her arms out, and yawned. Cautiously she looked across the dew-covered grass toward the still dark forest. Not a movement or a sound, did she see, or hear, just silence. Strange, there was no sign of life, no birds, no deer, no scurrying of little mice among the leaves.

Why was she here, and just where, was here? This place looked nothing like where she had been born. Confused, she looked around wondering.

Dawn started to break, dark and dreary, it looked like rain. Suddenly chilled and shivering she thought, *I'm not dressed for this.* With her magical powers, she created a black leather jumper laced up the front and trimmed with white fur, thick white leggings and knee-high black boots. In case it did rain, a black ankle length cape with a hood and pockets, which should keep her dry.

Making sure she was alone, she peered about, then removed and discarded her gown, tossing it carelessly onto the ground. She then proceeded to dress in her newly created clothes. Walking to a small grey boulder, she sat upon it, and with some effort pulled on the boots. "There, that should keep the cold from me." she said.

Looking up, the grey clouds were transforming into white fluffy ones, which were being blown rapidly toward the horizon. The sky was starting to clear. One stone stood out, it sat in the midst of the many varying shaped and size of grey boulders. Strangely, out of place, it was black and tall. It pointed ominously toward the sky like a bony finger.

Curiosity getting the better of her, she stood, looked around making sure it was safe, and took a couple of steps toward the black rock. It seemed so out of place. Why would a tall thin obelisk be here among all these grey boulders?

With this question in mind, she walked forward to investigate. As she drew closer, she saw something shiny partially buried in the dirt at its base. She bent down and scraped some of the dirt away. Something was there. Grasping an edge, she tugged and pulled at the metal object until it came free from the earth.

Standing she brushed more dirt from the object, and then turned to tap it against the obelisk to remove the rest of the dirt. As she looked at the aged and weather-beaten black stone obelisk, she noticed old letters hewed into the stones rough surface. The object in her hand was forgotten for the moment. She reached out in wonder with her fingers to brush the crusted dirt from the letters to better read them and touched the cold stone.

The instant her fingers touched the black stone she received a severe jolt of energy that lasted only a millisecond, but which sent her to her knees. Stunned and dizzy, she paused a moment and took several deep breaths. Her eyes blurry, she tried to focus, shaking her head to clear it. Not touching the stone, she wondered what had happened.

She stood looking down at the carved letters on the stone. The dirt and weathered abuse the stone had endured for who knows how long, made it difficult to read. She tried anyway. Unaware her lips were moving, she read aloud.

One will come...
To save country and kingdom
Blown in on a dark night's wind
Down to earth like an angel
On wings of white gossamer
Having the sweet innocence of a child

Fearing nothing... and no one

Standing there, still in a daze, she wondered what it meant.

Recovering from the jolt she'd received, she brushed a wisp of hair from her face, bent and picked up the object she'd dropped. Holding it up, she looked closely at it. What an odd shaped thing it was. What could it be? Then slowly it dawned on her, what she held in her hand was a wonderfully old, large silver and gold key, attached to a short, silver chain. She had never seen a key shaped as this one, or of such beauty. Surely, whoever owned it would not have thrown away such a key of this value. Someone must have lost it. She wondered what it fit and how it had ended up here.

Who could have lost this beautiful key?

Well, she might look for whoever lost it and return it to its rightful owner. Where should she start? How could she find them, that was the big question.

As she held the key, it slowly started to change shape. Morphing into an entirely different shape, the key was still beautiful, but different. Startled and amazed, but not afraid, she wondered how this could be. Was the key alive? She did not sense an entity, or was it some form of magic. Maybe it was cursed, or enchanted, or maybe it was under some sort of spell.

Holding the beautiful key in her hand, she turned away from the black obelisk a puzzled expression on her face. Startled, she dropped the key, almost fainting.

Chapter 2

a Friend ~ Love

Her heart beat rapidly from surprise. Shocked, she instinctively raised her hands in a stance of self-defense. Her mouth dry, she tried to speak, but no words came, only a garbled noise. With a lump in her throat, she was barely able to stutter, "Who?... who... Where did you come from?" she said as she took a quick step back.

Standing not more than three feet away, stood the most strikingly handsome male, she had seen in her sixteen short years. Just an inch over six feet, bronzed skin, his long silver hair drawn back and fastened with a sliver-clasped chain. He towered well over her short five-foot stature. She looked up into the most unusual captivating eyes, which were a golden-yellow. She had never seen such eyes of that color before.

How long had he been standing there, she wondered, and how had he been able to get this close without her knowing? He was dressed in a short black tunic, over loose fitted grey pants, belted at the waist with a wide black leather belt, held in place by a large silver buckle. The buckle glowed strangely, with an iridescent radiance. It caught and held Miiliinda's eyes momentarily.

He stared into her eyes. He did not speak nor move. His golden eyes held her tight. She was unable to move as if in a trance. He stood so still. Unblinking, he seemed like a statue to her, instead of flesh and blood.

After several moments, she felt a slight tingle, which started slowly in her head and then spread throughout her cold body, warming it. Then slowly at first, then faster and faster, the thoughts poured into her mind. *Not her thoughts, they must be his.* She felt warm. A feeling of peacefulness cursed throughout her body, all fear of this being before her were gone.

Somehow, his thoughts held something strange. A feeling of great sadness was scattered among them, a sadness she could not quiet place. Even though she tried her hardest, she could not break through, to the reason for his sadness.

Now that she was no longer afraid, she looked more closely at him. A handsomely rugged face that held in it a great sadness, a troubled face that showed tiredness on it, especially around his golden eyes. She took a step closer to this man, which she had been so afraid of only a second before, but was now so strangely attracted to. She found herself reaching out, and touching his hand wanting to comfort him. She asked, "Why are you so sad?"

He looked down at her, his bright golden eyes held her tight in their hypnotic gaze. Finally moving, he spoke in a language she could not understand. With her powers, she quickly transformed his words, into words she could understand without effort.

"You remind me of someone..." Tightness edged his voice. "Someone I once knew." His eyes filled with tears. He paused, reached up and brushed the tears from his eyes. "I'm sorry." he said. He looked back at her and then continued on, speaking softly in a slightly accented but stronger voice. "Someone I knew, in a different place and time."

He paused, swallowed hard, then continued on, "I don't like to think about it, but sometimes,... Sometimes, something or someone comes along which reminds me of her. Which in turn, compels me to keep searching for a way; I keep thinking there must be some way in which to set Emerauld free." He paused, and then sat on a small boulder, resting his head between his hands. He looked down deep in thought, remembering.

She noticed her pile of discarded garments as she waited for him to continue. *That's not like me*, she thought. Then she smiled, said a few magical words, and with a slight wave of her small hand, the garments vanished. Then she noticed the enchanted key she had dropped.. She bent down picked up the key and quickly slipped it into the pocket of her black cape.

If she could get him to talk, it might help cheer him. Moving closer, she reached out, taking his hand, she squeezed it. Then looked up and asked, "Do you want to tell me about it? Or, if it's to painful... would you rather not?"

Rubbing his forehead, he glanced at the forest, searching the shadows for an answer. "I suppose it wouldn't hurt to explain my pain." Then he brightened, "Perhaps, you could be of some help."

Suddenly, without warning, he turned away. He clenched his fist, and raised his arm toward the clearing overcast sky. In despair, he angrily shook his fist, and yelled at the dark clouds. "Damn you! Queen Gurold! A curse be cast upon you."

Turning back, he said in a somewhat controlled voice, "It will take awhile to tell my story, and to explain my predicament... quite a bit of time... I'm sure... And, I am sorry for the outburst."

She said, "There is no need for you to apologize. From the pained look on your face it is clear you are very frustrated." Shaking her head she asked, "Who is this Queen... This 'Queen Gurold' that you hate so very much? Is she the cause of all your distress?"

"Yes! She is.... But it is Emerauld I think about for most of my waking time." Then his expression changed. "Oh, but wait. You must forgive me. Here we have been talking for a lengthy period of time. You must certainly be hungry by now. After being dropped like a cat, in the middle of the night, into this dreary place. It must surely be far past the time for you to eat."

Shocked, an incredulous look of disbelief flickered across her face. "How do you know, I was dropped?"

He said, "I know a lot of things." as if addressing a child. "I was watching and waiting for you."

"You were! How did you know I was coming?"

"I knew someone would come. I did not know it would be you. That was what I meant. Can we not eat now, and discuss the matter later."

Putting a hand on her stomach, she said, "Now that you speak of food, my stomach does seem to be rumbling. Probably we should eat." Laughing, she flipped her long hair away from her face, and said, "So, kind sir, what are we to eat?" she glanced about at the dark forbidding forest. "I don't see anything we can eat, where are we to get food?"

A smile lit his face. He held a slightly calloused hand up to quiet her chatter. Then with a twinkle in his eye, he took a few steps into the meadow and stopped. Uttering a few words, he extending his arms outward, and with a great flourish of his hands, there suddenly appeared, spread wide across the grass on an elaborately woven carpet of red and gold, a banquet of luscious fruits on large silver platters. Everything a person might wish to partake of was there. Adorned with short blue tassels, several, large red pillows, were scattered about, which one could sit, or recline, as your mood wished.

He turned to her; a captivating smile had replaced the sadness. "You are not the only one with powers. I have a few also." He made a cavalier bow with a sweeping gesture of an arm. Chivalrously, he extended his hand, grasped hers gently, and said, "If it pleases milady, our banquet awaits, shall we eat."

Miiliinda sat on a pillow with her legs crossed. She reached out and taking a grape from a cluster, plopped it into her mouth. "I don't think anyone will disturb us, in this dark gloomy forest, do you?" She asked, chewing on her mouthful of grapes. Without waiting for his reply, "I love stories. I can hardly wait to hear yours, but my patience is almost gone. I am so very curious, please, do tell it." She implored, pushing another grape into her already full mouth. She leaned sideways against another pillow and made herself comfortable. She swallowed and asked "Who is this Emerauld, you talk of?" she asked, plopping another grape.

He held up his hand again and trying his best to calm her, said. "Yes, I see you have a lot of questions. However, please, try to be patient. First, I have questions of my own. Why were you dropped in the middle of night into my forest?" He looked questioningly at her for an answer. "And who are you? If you answer my questions, then maybe, I will tell my story... maybe. What is your name, and where did you come from, and why."

Chewing another grape, she rose and stretching, tilted her head and looked down upon the stranger, who reclined across a large pillow. With a crooked smile on her lips and a gleam in her eye, she began. "My name is Miiliinda. I come from a land far across the sea, a small island called Chinnder. A wonderfully enchanted beautiful land, with flowering trees, and plants, and streams, and rivers, with lots of lakes, and ponds filled with fish, of ever color. It's not at all like this dreary, forsaken place." Running out of breath, she quickly took a deep breath, and continued. "Furthermore, I don't know why I am here. I was hoping maybe you could tell me. I wish someone would help me on that point." She finished exuberantly.

Laughing, he sat up and exclaimed, "For such a little girl you sure can say a lot with one breathe. You might try speaking slower. Do you always speak that fast?" he asked smiling.

Embarrassed, she turned a slight shade of pink and replied. "No, only when I'm excited or nervous."

"And which are you now, excited or nervous?" His voice was inquisitive, but his eyes were laughing at her.

She ignored the question, glanced at the forest then at the ground and said, "Now you know all about me and I know nothing of you," she said, trying to avoid his question. Without pausing she continued, "May I ask, who are you and what is your name,? What were you doing out in the middle of the night, in this cold dark and eerie forest?"

"You ask a lot of questions for such a young girl. But yes, we are after all, sort of getting to know one another, aren't we."

Showing a trait of stubbornness and shaking a finger at him, she angrily replied, "I am not a young girl, I am sixteen, and in my country most girls my age are married."

Standing and folding his bare arms across his broad chest, he looked straight into her eyes and said, "I am known as Alaric." For a fleeting instant, a pained expression flitted across his face. Becoming quiet, he said nothing more, deep in thought.

"That's it?... You're only going to tell me just your name and nothing more. That's not right or fair, what about your story you were going to tell!" she shouted.

"That is all you need to know at this time, my sweet little one."

Losing her temper, she started pounding on his chest with two small fists. She yelled, "I am not your sweet little one, and don't call me that, I don't even know you!"

"Calm down," He said, grabbing her hands. "I was only teasing. You're so animated when you get angry. It is such fun watching your expressions change, If you want to hear my story, I will tell you... Just stop beating on my chest."

"Oh, sorry," She stopped pounding on his chest, which really had not bothered him at all. "Please do forgive me, but you really do make me mad." Then with a sparkle to her eye, she said. "Now that that's out of the way, I can't wait. Who is this person Emerauld that you speak of? Please do tell me," she implored, "Please, Alaric, I am so very curious."

Alaric tugged on his ear, paused, thoughtfully for a moment, then rubbed his chin and said, "Unless I start at the very beginning it would not make sense. It is a complicated tale, so please, let me relate my experiences. How should I begin?"

Chapter 3

journeys ~ a Beggar ~ Treasure
Alaric's ... story

When I was younger and more adventurous, I traveled to many places and cities, in many deferent countries, in search of treasure. Which sometimes, on rare occasion, I found. But other times, I found, I had just wasted my time.

I walked down the wind blown dusty street of the city looking for something. I didn't know for what I looked, but when I found it, I would know. A clue maybe. It was one of many cities on my list to visit. This one was old and neglected.

Holding onto the brim of my hat, I leaned into the blowing dust. The heat of the sun beat down cruelly. My shirt wet with sweat clung to me. Thirsty, I looked for a place to get out of the wind and wash the dirt from my throat. Someplace where I could get a cool drink and think. I glanced up and down the street if you could call it that.

Luck was with me. Down the dingy street on my left, a sign stuck out from a storefront. I could barely read it through the blowing dust, it read, 'Rest and Drinks.' Normally it would have taken me some time to find a place.

Entering and sitting at a low counter, my eyes adjusted from the bright sun to the dimly lit room. I removed my hat, pulled a bandanna from my pocket, and wiped the sweat from my forehead. The place was mostly empty except for three loud men that were waving their hands madly about. They seemed to be deep in a heated discussion.

A bald man with a worn tunic open at the throat, showing a patch of curly dark hair, stood behind the counter. He approached and said, "The punch is good." While he stood waiting for an answer, he wiped at the counter with a rag that was as dirty as the tunic he wore. In a thick voice he continued. "It is what most people order in this drinking place. If you want, I can also add different things to the punch... to give it more punch." He said laughing, at his joke. I ordered a cool glass of punch from the man with the dirty tunic.

I sat sipping on my punch, which was surprisingly not half bad. I begin to relax from the hot sun. I glanced slowly around surveying the room. My gaze came to rest on three shabbily dressed men, at a nearby table. They still appeared to be in some sort of heated argument. From their condition and loudness of their voices, it appeared they had had too much of the *good* punch.

Occasionally, I would catch a word. My curiosity getting the best of me, I listened more closely, trying to make out what was said. Then I heard the words *treasure* and *cave* in the same sentence.

Calling the tavern keeper over I said that I would like to buy the three men a drink. Upon serving the drinks at the table, he pointed in my direction, and the three men turned and stared at me for a moment, and then raised their mugs to my good health. Turning back, they started arguing amongst themselves again. Then one turned and gestured for me to join them, which was what I'd wanted all along.

Picking up my drink, I moved to their table. After a few sips and names being passed around, they returned to the argument. Accepting me into their group, they continued their heated conversation, bickering and quarreling. I sat and listened.

The fattest of the three was relating to the others that he had heard an old tale, of a cave that held a great treasure, located on a mountainside somewhere. He didn't know where. It would bring to whoever found it, great wealth and riches beyond their wildest dreams.

My interest was now greatly aroused. Trying to get as much information as possible, I asked many questions about where this cave might be. No one knew. That's why they had been arguing. It was just a story they all seemed to have heard. One of the men thought that it really existed. The other two men argued and said, *"It's just a fantasy."* If it were real, surely someone would have stumbled upon it by now.

I had visited several nearby cities which had mountains, which I had explored their numerous caves in my quest for this mysterious cave, of which the three had spoken. At the end of several fruitless months, I had discovered nothing. Disheartened and weary, by the long search, for a fabled cave which eluded me. I was beginning to believe it really was just a story, with no truth to it. Still, I was not ready to give up.

~ ~ ~

After a long dusty carriage ride, I arrived at the city of Pacort. It was the last city on my list. I began a search, for clues, rumors, or anything, that might point me in the right direction. I was determined and hoped to find something, anything, before giving up and taking a short rest from my searching.

I awoke to the sounds of the city early the next day with a clear head, a better attitude and rested after a good nights sleep. I listen to the sounds of dogs barking, shutters banging open, people calling out to one another, and peddlers hawking their wares as I dressed.

Stepping from the hotel, I ventured forth among its citizens. I observed most were poorly dressed. I started the day by asking questions, discretely of course. I didn't want any treasure seekers, if there were any, to be aware of a stranger asking about a long lost fabled cave which held great treasures.

I talked with several people, old and young and was getting nowhere in my queries. I stopped and looked curiously around at the buildings of every shape and size. Some were new, but most were old and run down.

A warm breeze had sprung up and was blowing the dust. I slowly walked across the dusty street shielding my eyes from the dust, while dodging carts, and people going in all directions.

As I approached the other side, my eyes were drawn to a building that seemed oddly out of place. Stuck between two newer buildings, was an old run down, dilapidated, store, with a sign hanging crookedly by one rusted chain from the buildings front. From where I stood, some distance off, I could not read it. I walked closer, in spite of all the grime and dirt with which it was coated; I was able to make out the words, '*Books for Sale*' and underneath in smaller words, *some old, some new.*

A thought suddenly occurred to me. Maybe, just maybe, someone had written something about the cave for which I searched. Getting my hopes up, I took a step forward opened the door and stepped inside. I stood dumbfounded by what I saw - a quaint old bookstore. My eyes slowly became accustom to the dim light which filtered in through the dirty window. I stood there looking around not knowing what I could or would find. As my eyes adjusted to the dark interior, I picked up a book, and blew the dust from its cover. I noticed everything in the store was covered with dust.

A curtain rustled, as it was brushed aside, and I was greeted by an old man as dirty as the store. He shuffled up. "You come to buy book, no?" he said, with a wide toothless grin.

My nose twitched, assaulted by the smell of dust, mildew and other odors, which I could not identify. Trying not to breathe, I said, "Maybe—it depends." I paused, looked around at the disarray of dusty books, some on shelves, and some stacked haphazardly about, on the dirty tile floor. I guessed there must have been thousands.

"How do you find anything in all this cluttered mess?"

"Oh! I find any thing you want." he said, still grinning. He waved his arm toward the many books around the room then slapped his hand down on a book and sent dust flying in ever direction. "What you want?"

Choking and coughing, I waved one hand through the air trying my best to dissipate the dust. Stifling an urge to sneeze, I raised the other to my nose and mouth, and asked, "Have you any books on caves... old caves... caves that might have been discovered long ago, written about, and then forgotten about?"

"Aha! I think I know of what you look. But you cannot find in book," he said, scratching his head and looking straight at me. "Pray to my mother, but why do you wish such a book?"

I tried to explain. "I am an explorer of caves and I have been looking for a particular cave, which it seems, I can not find. It has eluded me for many months. However, I am determined sooner or later, I will find it. I was hoping maybe to find a clue or some further description leading to its location... and I will not give up my looking."

"Ah! Yes, yes... but you say nothing of riches that awaits the finder of cave. Let me think, if I can remember the rumors." He tugged at his beard a moment, then suddenly looked up. "Yes I remember now. I believe it was called the 'Crystal Cave.' It was said the riches it contained was beyond any thing a man can dream. It could make a man a king. It could make several men kings. The riches indeed must be extraordinary. I too have heard such a story. Sometimes I wonder, does such a cave exist, or maybe only a fantasy But then... as you can see, I am only a poor shopkeeper, and far too old to look for It."

"If such a cave were to exist it seems to me someone would have found it by now. You could not keep such a thing secret for long. It seems that your search in this city will be in vain." He paused, closed his eyes and mumbled something to himself. Opening his eyes he said, "If I were to tell you what I remember, it might be of some use to you, yes? Perchance you could compensate me with a small token of appreciation, yes.

My interest was *piqued;* I had to know what this old man might know. "Please," I begged, "If you know of anything that would be of help, I possibly could give a token of gratitude, if I deem the information worthwhile. Moreover, I would forever be in your debt and I most certainly would not forget."

He scratched his beard, while he thought about what I had said. "Well," he started. "A few years back, there was some talk that outside the city of Borrgess, on a mountain some distance from the city, was a cave such as you seek. I should also warn you." he said as he stroked his beard.

"Warn me of what?"

"The King and Queen."

"What about the King and Queen?" I asked.

"King Barubus rules our country, and his wife Queen Gurgold, rules the king. Most of the people in Borrgess hate the King and Queen, who live in high splendor, in a grand castle built high on the rolling hills above the lowly citizens of the city. Mostly though, they hate the Queen and her high taxes which they are compelled to pay. They are an impoverished people. The tax the people are burdened with is so great there is very little left for them to exist on. For those that don't pay, they are thrown into the castle dungeon. Few survive with the rats and the very little food they are given."

"Further, there are those in the kingdom who say..." stopping, he looked fearfully about to see if anyone could hear and whispered, "She is a witch. Not only do they say she is a witch and sorceress, but a dark witch of the underworld. One does not cross her and live very long. Borrgess is about a three-day's journey from here. Perhaps you maybe should go there to continue your search."

With a last parting remark he said, "When you arrive in Borrgess, keep a low profile and tread carefully my friend, for she has eyes everywhere and knows everything that goes on in Borrgess."

I listened, deep in thought as the bearded old shopkeeper spoke. I looked at him for a moment. "Thank you, you have been most helpful." I placed a coin in his open palm. "I will tread lightly my friend, and try not to bring undue attention my way."

I stepped out the door into bright sunshine. Briefly, for a moment I stood thinking. Yes, what the old man had said seemed very promising. I would go to this city they called Borrgess.

~ ~ ~

Upon my arrival in the city of Borrgess and not knowing how long my stay would be, I set about looking for lodging. It was a short search. I found a nondescript three-story structure on a side street, at the edge of the city. After getting settled, I spent the next few days, discreetly prying and snooping for information or a clue, which might lead me to the cave I was seeking.

One hot afternoon, taking time from my quest, I sat at a small, round table, in front of a small street café, shaded somewhat by an umbrella that sprouted from its center. I watched the citizens going about their daily business, while I sipped on a cool drink. They walked slowly along the dusty street, seemingly unaffected by the scorching hot sun.

My eyes were busy taking in all the activity, when I noticed a dirty, ragged beggar. He sat in the dirt, leaning against an old wooden wheel, of a broken down horse cart, begging for any thing a passer by might be willing to give.

I finished my drink and leaving the café, passed close by the beggar. I placed a one-Zoltar coin into the tin cup he held. He looked up blinking, teary bloodshot eyes, and nodding, he thanked me profusely.

Continuing on I suddenly had a hunch. Who better than a lowly beggar would know all the local gossip? I stopped and walked back. I took from my purse a ten-Zoltar coin. Holding it before the toothless beggar I asked, "Have you lived in this region long?"

Spitting into the dirt he looked at the coin through his bloodshot eyes. At sight of the coin, his face lit up and he excited replied, in a gravelly voice. "Yes, I... I was born here, why do you ask?"

"So, you should be familiar with the area and the out lying country?"

"Yes, Yes," drooling, he reached for the coin.

I pulled the coin back and smiled. "Not so fast. To earn this, you must give me some answers. Have you ever heard anyone talk or tell of a long lost secret cave somewhere around here?"

He replied with a grunt, "Let me see," and closed his eyes for several seconds thinking. "Yes, it comes to me now. It was said that several years ago, a man came down from a mountain that lies on the far side of the great river Weettan. He drowned trying to cross the river. They found his body late one day, stiff and dead, washed up on the riverbank. They found clutched in his lifeless hand a stone of great beauty."

He paused and thought—then continued speaking. "In the past many people have gone into those mountains looking for where the stone had come from. Some came back empty handed and some did not come back at all. No one seems to know what happened to the ones that never returned. But no one, so far as I know, has ever found anything worthwhile."

"There are several mountains in the area you describe. Can you be a little more precise in identifying which mountain you are referring to?" I asked.

"Everyone who talked to me seemed to think it is the largest of a group of three mountains. It is called 'Zantarre.' Because they are so close together the local people call them The Three Sisters," he said looking up. "And it is said that our god has forsaken those mountains by giving them only a few plants and fewer trees, the rest being covered with rocks and boulders. That is what I have heard. Those mountains are the place where the treasure must be. That is the rumor I have heard for all these years. No one knows for sure, since, no one has returned with jewels. No one has found the fabled cave... yet."

Dropping the ten-zoltar coin into his cup, I thanked him. "You have been most helpful,"

"May Zarnn the goddess of luck, bless and guide you on your quest," he replied, making a Z motion with his hand.

The beggar watched as I walked away. I decided to try my luck, on this mountain called Zantarre of which he spoke.

Chapter 4

Tagg

First thing I should do. Purchase enough supplies to last at least a month, and probably a horse for me to ride and a mule for carrying the supplies. Not knowing the city and being new here, I stopped a young couple and asked where I might purchase supplies for a trip around the countryside. I made no mention of the mountains where I would begin my search for the lost cave. They directed me to 'Vaadars' which they said was down the street and part way through an alley walk way. It was not a good part of the city they said, but Vaadar was an honest and fair supplier of goods. Their parting words to me were, "Be careful."

It seemed odd to me that everywhere I went, every person I spoke with, all said, 'Be careful.' I wondered what I was to be careful of.

Following the directions, I had been given; I finally arrived at a store that matched the rest of the old buildings in this run down part of town. A small sign on the front of the building read, 'Vaadar's Trading and Bartering.' The people were right; this was not a good part of the city.

Several men of doubtful intent sat around on some old crates, idling their time away talking. A few more leaned with elbows resting on the crates. The men stopped talking in mid conversation as I walked up. Silent they stared at me, intently. Several ragged young boys were playing a game in the dirt beside the front door. The boys stopped playing the games. All eyes were directed towards me, as I stepped up on the porch and opened the door. I noticed one of the boys that had stopped his playing, was watching me with great curiosity.

Stepping inside I was greeted by a giant of a man with a belly that almost matched his height. He squinting at the glare from the open doorway and stroking a long black beard, asked with a voice deep as thunder, "What sir, might I do for you?"

I closed the door behind me and taking my hat off, I looked around the well-stocked store, before I answered. "I need supplies for a journey I'm planning."

"What kind of supplies?" he asked, between puffs on his pipe. "This journey you are planning. Will be short or long?"

"Well, I plan to be out around a month." This man was all business I could see. He was straightforward with few words. I liked that. "I'm not familiar with the countryside. You would know better what supplies I'd need for survival in this part of the country."

Taking the pipe from his mouth, he asked, "My friend how much do you wish to spend?"

"You select what you think I will need to last me for a month. If you go beyond the amount I can pay, I will stop you." I said rubbing my ear. "My name is Vaadar and what may I call you sir?"

I leaned over the counter and said, "You can call me Alaric."

"Well Alaric, being a fair man. I must tell you in advance, if we are to do business together you will need either a wagon or a mule to carry enough supplies to last you a month."

"Well, I am planning on traveling fast. I think maybe a wagon would slow me up to much. I was sort of thinking maybe a horse and a mule. What do you think?"

"My friend, if it were me, those would be the choices I'd make." He smiled, tugged at his beard and went on, "As fate would have it, I just happen to have two such fine animals. Would you like to buy them outright or use them for a fee?"

"You would not want me to decide before seeing them, would you?" Purchasing the supplies I needed and a few I thought might come in handy. I began to pack them into a new carrying pack. Vaadar watched as

I packed and asked, "Would you like to see the animals before or after you finish packing?"

I looked up from my packing. "It depends on where they are.

"In the stable just through the back door," he said, grinning.

"Well, if they're that close lets have a look at them."

"Please follow me," he said moving toward a door in the back.

Shoving the backpack down on the counter, I followed Vaadar out through the door. I had to step up onto a short wooden walkway that ran by a couple of stalls, holding two horses and a mule. One of the horses snorted, started kicking and jumping around nervously as we approached. "Sort of touchy isn't he!" I said, looking at a horse as black as midnight.

"Yes, but as you can see, he is a very fine, spirited horse. He can take you wherever you wish. And once he gets to know you he will calm down... that is, if he likes you." Then he roared, with a deep booming laugh.

"He is a fine looking horse and the mule looks able enough, how much for the two of them?"

"Well... let me see," Looking up at the stable roof he mumbled to himself, after a few quick calculations, "I guess you can have them for," again he paused, looked at my expression wonderingly, and rubbing his beard said, "Five hundred Zoltars."

Shaking my head, "I thought you were a fair man, that's far too many Zoltars, for just two animals."

"Yes! Ok! Can't blame one for trying," he gave me a good-natured grin. "How does four hundred and fifty Zoltars sound?"

"That's still too much."

"Ok!... My best price especially for you my good friend, three hundred ninety Zoltars."

I started to protest, but he continued on.

"And my friend, I will throw in the supplies, and the carrying pack, and even the equipment for the horse and mule."

"It's a deal," I said quickly, before he changed his mind.

"Let us go inside and finish with our agreement," He walked through the rear door, back into the store, with me close behind.

As I stepped through the doorway, my eye caught a glimpse over

Vaadar's shoulder of my carrying pack being dragged rapidly out the door which stood open, it disappeared around the corner. I yelled at the top of my lungs, "Hey you... Stop."

I dashed after the thief. My long legs pumping, I rounded the corner in five giant steps. The thief had not gotten far. His legs were too short and the pack was too heavy. Four more steps and I grabbed the thief by the neck. As I yanked him back, he let go of the carrying pack.

He screamed, "Let me go." Kicking and cursing he tried to hit me with his two small fists and yelled, "Let go."

I had to laugh at the little tiger I held squirming at arms length, and in the gruffest voice I could muster, asked, "Where do you think you were going my small friend?"

"Please mister, don't hurt me." Calming down he said, "I only wanted to trade it for some food." He looked up at me, as if defying me to hit him.

My hand tightened its grip on his skinny neck. "Look," I said, "I'm not going to hurt you. So why not try telling the truth."

He bent his head down, kicked at the dirt with his bare feet, not saying anything. He then looked back up at me and said, "Well I needed some shoes." He looked at me with a questioning expression to see if I was buying his second explanation.

I shook my head and had to smile, "Can't you come up with a better story than that?" I loosened my grip slightly.

"No. That's the only thing I can thing of right now," he said and shrugged his skinny shoulders in defeat.

"Ok, how about just the truth."

"Well," putting his hands up to partially cover his mouth he whispered in my ear. "See the man sitting on the black crate over there, he owns me." Tears starting to form in his eyes then welled over leaving streaks down his cheeks. "I have to do everything he says, or he will beat me."

"Is he your father?" I asked.

"No," He wiped at his eyes, using the sleeve of his dirty tattered shirt and said, "My father is in the debtors prison, and I don't know what's become of my mother." he said with a loud sigh. "She just left one day and never came back."

"Do you like the situation you're in?" I asked.

"What do you mean? I don't understand."

"Do you like your life the way it is?" I said.

"No... but what can I do? I'm only a kid."

"Would you like to end your relationship with that man?"

"Yes... I would do anything to be free from him, if only I could."

There was something about this kid which reminded me of myself at his age. I thought for a moment, and then said, "How would you like to come along with me? You could help in my travels."

"Truly, that would be great. If only I could. But he won't let me go."

"Don't worry kid. I will take care of that problem. It would surely please me, if you would take the carrying pack back into the store, and wait there for me." I said in a stern voice. Then I turned my attention toward the man sitting on the black crate.

Moments later, I walked back into the store. The kid was sitting on a small box, being lectured by Vaadar. Walking over I said. "Well it's all taken care of, you now belong to me."

"What, what happened?" the kid asked his eyes wide.

"I just convinced him he would be better off without you," Rubbing my knuckles, I smiled down at the kid. "My name is Alaric, and you now belong to me, what is your name?"

Looking up with hope in his eyes, he replied, "Everyone calls me Taggaloon."

"That's a pretty big name for such a small boy. "How old are you, or do you know?"

Laughing, he said, "Yes I do know. I am eight, almost nine and I can beat almost anyone twice my size, at anything." Throwing out his chest, he strutted about like a peacock.

"Taggaloon, you don't have to prove anything to me, I know you are *very* tough." I turned to Vaadar and said, "Vaadar, can you get the kid traveling clothes?"

"Yes, right away. Let's see what you need." He squinted, looking down at Taggaloon. "Get out of those dirty rags. You will need a complete, and I do mean completely new attire. Take off everything and put it in that box of garbage." he said waving to a box setting by the front door.

While Taggaloon did as he was told. Vaadar was removing shirt, pants, boots and a hat from the shelf behind the counter. Turning back, he placed the items quickly on the counter "There that should be everything you need." He said, rubbing his hands in anticipation, thinking of the extra money to be paid for the change of clothes.

Taggaloon, naked, grabbed the clothes as quickly as they were being placed on the counter and started putting them on. When he finished dressing, he smiled.

Alaric held Taggaloon at arms length and turned him around, "What a difference, you look like a new man.

"Taggaloon smiled. "Yes, I feel very good... but...

"But what," I said, a note of exasperation edging into my stern voice.

"It's just that... I really do like these clothes... it's just that," pausing, he looked down the counter and said; "I really, really would like that shiny new knife over there. If it were mine, I would be able to protect myself and you."

"Do you think you could protect me from a ten-foot giant?" I said, teasingly, with a laugh.

"Yes, sir, I would cut off his toes and when he bent over I could cut him good."

"Okay, kid, you talked me into it." I looked at Vaadar, shrugged my shoulders, and said, "I guess you just sold a knife. I'll take the one the kid wants and maybe it would be a good idea that I get one also. Just in case. I'll take the long one next to it and a couple of sheaths to hold them."

"Come on kid, let's get out of here before I spend all my Zoltars," I said, as I finished paying Vaadar what was owed.

Stepping outside I stopped and looked at the kid, and said, "Look kid, I can't keep calling you kid and Taggaloon is just a mouthful too much to say. Don't people call you something besides Taggaloon or kid?"

"They call me everything," he said frowning.

"How about we just shorten your name to... let me think, how does Tagg sound to you?"

"Tagg... Tagg," he said. "Yeah, it sounds okay. I kind of like it."

"Okay, Tagg it is. And you, you can stop calling me sir. Call me Alaric. "Okay," Tagg said and smiled.

Chapter 5

an Angry Earth

After helping the kid up onto the mule, I turned to the skittish black stallion. He tried to pull away. I mounted quickly and he was not at all happy, with me or my added weight. Jumping quickly to the left, then right, he arched his back and tried to toss me. I looked at Tagg; his eyes had become large as saucers. Then he grinned. With strong hands and a gentle, soothing voice, the stallion calmed and slowly settled down.

The mule stood quiet, watching the antics of the horse. Once everything was under control, we moved off. The first hour we rode slowly, me getting a feel for the horse and his playful personality. Tagg having never ridden before was all smiles as he became use to the mule and mule to him.

In a good mood, my hopes high, we traveled out and away from the city, to begin our great adventure in search for the fabled cave. Once the animals became accustomed to carrying us, their pace quickened. They were eager to go. I had planed to travel light and fast, but that was before Tagg. The mule was just slightly shorter than the horse, and strong, even burdened with a kid and supplies, it seemed not to bother him, so we made good time in our journey.

We traveled for several days through a changing land seeing not one living soul. It was devoid of all life except for that which crawled on it. Then one day we came upon a vast plain covered with short brush, huge boulders and a few trees. Moving slowly we worked our way through this tangle of brush and trees. Following the directions I had been given, as best as I could remember them.

Losing our way only once and stirring up good amount of dust getting back to the trees which were becoming fewer and further apart. We rode, weaving our way in and out around huge boulders and working our way slowly through jagged rocks, which covered a gradually upward slope, we traveled on in a westerly direction.

Reaching the top of a ridge, I saw in the far distance several mountains. My breath quickened and with my heart pounding, I counted their peaks. There was only one problem, there were more than the three mountains, I had been told about. I sat there dumbfounded on the stallion and counted five peaks that I could see, as the sun moved down and merged into the horizon.

I stopped and dismounted from the stallion, which I'd started calling Diablo, because of his spicy temperament. I slapped the dust from my pants and rubbed my rear, thinking.

Tagg pulled up a couple of seconds later and jumped off of the mule. He looked at me with a questioning expression on his face. "Boss... ah... Alaric, why are we stopping here?"

"There were only supposed to be three mountains, now there are five." I said, removing my hat and scratching my head. "It seems we could have us a slight problem."

"So, do we have to explore all the mountains?" Tagg asked, rolling his eyes. "It could be fun, couldn't it? Why are we looking for one certain mountain? What's so special about it anyway?"

"Oh, that's right; I didn't tell you when you got caught stealing my supplies. Well, I explore caves because I like it and sometimes I even find treasure."

"It sounds scary going into a dark cave... Is it dangerous... are there snakes?" Tagg asked.

"Sometimes it can be dangerous, but most of the time its not. You just have to be careful and use your head." I held up my hand in a gesture for silence. "Listen, do you hear anything?"

Tagg cocked his head and listened. "What am I listening for, I don't hear anything."

"Don't you hear it? It sounds like water flowing over rocks or maybe a waterfall."

"Yes, you're right, I hear it now. It seems to be coming from beyond that next ridge." Tagg said getting excited.

Mounting up we started toward the sound. The animals started acting up and moving faster as we drew closer. Cresting the ridge, we looked down on a roaring and swiftly moving river, as it rushed past. We slowed the animals to a walk, and as we approached the river we stopped, and just sat, staring at the wildly, churning, muddy waters. What a sight it was. This must be the mighty river Weettan, that had claimed the life of the man they'd found clutching the jewel. No wonder he didn't make it across, this had to be the largest river I had ever seen.

Looking around, I said, "We will make camp next to those two large boulders over there. And tonight let us think about what our next move will be."

The next morning we were jolted awake. A great rumbling sound followed by the earth shaking. Instantly, I jumped to my feet and started to calm the animals, as the earth continued to shake and roll beneath me.

I yelled, "Tagg! Help me with the animals."

While we struggled to hold them, the earth finally stopped shaking. The air was heavy with dust, making it hard to breath. Rocks and dirt-covered boulders were strewn about as if tossed like marbles from a giant hand.

"What was that?" Tagg asked, a frightened look on his face.

"I don't know, but whatever it was I didn't like it. Someone in the past remarked to me that he'd been in a situation where the earth shook and grumbled. He thought it was perhaps, because the earth was not happy with him. I don't think the earth is unhappy with us. What do you think?" I ask Tagg.

He replied trying to look thoughtful and grown up. "Well, I don't know, but I sure don't want to go through that again. It knocked me down, and when I tried to stand up, it knocked me down again."

"Yes, it was something which I hope not to repeat. Are you okay, you're not hurt are you?"

"No, I don't think so," Tagg replied shaking his head, feeling his arms and legs. "I think everything is okay."

While the dust settled, I caught my breath and looked around. More boulders were pushed up out of the ground along with a new jagged ridge running out away from the river. Otherwise, the land had not changed much. The horse and mule had quieted and seemed to be alright.

Turning toward Tagg I said, "Let's pack up and get the hell out of here before another one of those things occurs."

"I'm all for that!" he replied and started packing the mule.

Packed up and saddled, we hurriedly departed. We made our way hastily through the jumbled mess of boulders. The air was still heavy with settling dust. We made our way slowly down to the river and stopped.

"It sure is wide. How are we going to get to the other side?" Tagg asked tentatively.

"That's a good question." Hands on my hips, I stood looking across the river, it must have been at least a hundred feet bank to bank. I looked up and down the swiftly flowing muddy waters of the deadly river. "We could travel upstream toward its source, it probably will get somewhat narrower and we can perchance find a better place to cross."

We headed up river towards a newly formed jagged ridge which the earth had pushed up. As we got closer, it appeared much larger than I had at first thought. It surely must be fifteen to twenty feet high. Gritting my teeth, I thought. How are we ever going to get over it? Maybe we could go around it, if it didn't extend to far from the river.

I squinted along the length of the ridge hoping to see its end, there was a chance maybe we could go around it to the other side. My heart sunk as the ridge appeared to go on forever. What else could happen!

Suddenly, without warning the earth gave a shudder that was short and ended almost as soon as it started. It was over before I could react. I looked at the insurmountable ridge, still some distance away. Parts of it had started cracking and pieces begin to fall, hitting the ground. "Maybe there's an opening large enough for us to traverse to the far side." I said, looking hopefully at Tagg. "Let's go take a look.

"Tagg started to say something then stopped. His face was pale and he chewed on his lower lip.

"Your not going to let a little jolt like that frighten you?" I said, putting an arm around his shoulders.

He shrugged. "No it just surprised me is all." he said with a show of bravado.Minutes later, we arrived at the slide. Several loose rocks tumbled down filling the air with dust. Staying well clear if more rocks were to come down, we surveyed the scene and waited for the dust to clear. What we saw was disappointing. The slide had not presented a way over or through to the other side.

Cursing in disgust, I took off my hat and slung it to the ground. "I'm sorry, I didn't mean to curse. It seems all I have is bad luck." I said, picking up a grapefruit size rock and hurling it as hard as I could at the slide. It hit hard and started to roll down, and with it, the slide started to move.

Jumping clear we stood and watched as more and more of the ridge fell away. Finally, it stopped sliding. Waiting for the dust to clear I picked up my hat, shook the dirt from it and stuck it back on my head. Sitting down upon a small boulder, I just stared at the slide that still didn't make a way for us.

Tagg walked over and put his arm around my neck. "Don't worry. You will think of someway to get us across the river."

Standing, I walked to the horse, got my canteen from the saddle, and took a large swallow of water to get rid of the dust and dirt in my mouth. "Tagg, want a drink?"

Chapter 6

the White Wolf ~ a River to Cross

Miiliinda stood, and opened her mouth to ask a question. Alaric stopped in the midst of telling his story. Quickly he held up a hand stopping her words. "I know what your about to say. You're wondering why I didn't use my magical powers to cross the river. You see, I was only a normal man at that time, without any magical powers at all.

Miiliinda started to speak, "Well... Her sudden shriek drew his attention. "Stop! There I saw it again!" She exclaimed.

With a questioning look in his eyes, Alaric looked at her. Somewhat perturbed at being interrupted he stopped his adventure telling and said, "You saw what again?" He looked in the direction she was pointing. "I see nothing, what did you see?" he said, looking into the forest.

"The same white flash I saw shortly after landing last night. It was moving so fast I only caught a glimpse from the corner of my eye. I thought at first I was imagining things, but I saw it again just now. Did you not see it?" she asked hopeful.

"No—I did not see anything. What did it look like?"

"I could not tell, it moved too fast. I think it might have been an animal of some kind, but I'm not sure."

Alaric thought for a moment. He looked up at the forest again in time to see a flash of white moving along inside the edge of the forest. Looking closer, he studied it carefully and saw that it was a white wolf, playing along the edge of the trees. How best could he explain the flash she had seen was a white wolf---without frightening her?

"What kind of animal can move that fast?" She asked a little hesitantly. "It could be upon us in an instant and rip us apart. What should we do? Should we cast a spell of magic? I know I said a lot of things earlier about all my powers. But I'm not so sure how to use some of them, since I only recently acquired them." she shrugged her shoulders and forced a fearful smile. "This is your country can't you protect us if it were to attack?"

"It is nothing, probable only an animal looking for something to eat." He said trying to reassure her. "Don't worry, it's alright."

"Maybe he thinks we are his breakfast." she said, her voice shaky. Then she saw it plainly. A large white wolf moving in and out along the forest edge, then it turned and stared straight toward her. Miiliinda instinctively raised a hand to her mouth in fear. Becoming alarmed she edged closer to Alaric. Putting his arm protectively around her, Alaric reached out with his mind and touched the wolf.

"Stop now," he commanded. The wolf stopped, and looked out between the trees in their direction. *"Come to me,"* Alaric ordered. The wolf moved past a few trees to the tree line. It paused in the shadows then wary stepped out into the open, It looked carefully around, lowered his head to sniff the grassy ground, and stopped.

"Come to me now, my brother." Alaric sent his thought with more force. The wolf raised his head listening, and stared at them with black, yellow-edged eyes. He walked warily in their direction one slow step at a time. Apprehensively, he came closer, his slow steps becoming faster and faster. The slow walk changed suddenly into a burst of speed as he raced toward them, running so fast he became a streak of white.

Frantic with fear, Miiliinda screamed and clutched Alaric's arm. She thought surely they were being attacked. The wolf approached with such great speed, it ran past them like a whirlwind and then turned to make another charge. He came back running rings around them. He tired finely, stopped, and rolled over and over ending at Alaric's feet.

Alaric showed no fear. "Raddick, how are you my brother?" he reached down and as he stroked the wolf, a forlorn smile crossed his lips. He looked up. "Miiliinda, this is my younger brother."

"Do not worry little one, he will not harm you. Furthermore, while we are together, I will protect you from all things, living or dead."

She let go of his arm. "I told you don't call me your little one. I am not a child."

"Sometimes you do act like one."

Momentarily distracted, she asked, "What was that you said about the *living* or dead, particularly the part about the *dead?*"

"Don't worry about the dead. We'll have trouble enough, dealing with the living. Now let me finish the telling of my story. Then all your questions will be answered."

"Wait she exclaimed. What about this wolf at your feet, you call a brother?" The wolf looked up at her and whined. Then he stood and moved close to her and lay at her feet. Putting his large pointed nose on his front paws, he closed his eyes, contented.

"See he has taken to you. He would not harm you. He seems to care."

She knelt beside the wolf and cautiously placed a hand on the soft fur, her fear replaced by a warm feeling. A questioning look in her eyes, her lips parted to speak, she looked up at Alaric. "I have but one question about the story you are telling."

"Hush, Little one, the truth will be revealed in the story, now be quiet and listen."

Miiliinda shook her head and listened as Alaric said, "Now, where did I leave off? Oh yes I was about to tell of my search for the hidden cave."

~ ~ ~

I was so mad I had thrown a large rock at the ridge, the sliding of the rocks stopped and there appeared an opening. Stunned for a moment, I started toward the opening that held a soft golden-yellow glow about its edges. Tagg followed close on my heels. His mouth hung open as did mine.

The opening looked to be on fire, but I felt no heat. I reached the jagged opening and hesitantly reached out and touched an edge. It was cold to my touch. Peering inside it appeared to be a tunnel of sorts, such as a giant worm might make. If it was made by a giant worm, I hoped not to encounter it.

I stepped through the opening and once inside, I looked down this strange rounded structure. The walls were smooth, but had a rippled sheen that glowed, casting forth a yellow light. It stretched as far as my eye could see. My faith in the gods was restored. This could be the way to cross the river, or to better put it, under the river. I would soon find out.

The horse and mule balked at the opening, neither wanted to enter. With some effort and much coaching, we slowly got the animals through the opening into the large glowing passageway, once inside both animals calmed and settled somewhat. Being careful and not knowing what to expect or what might lie ahead, I led the way on foot. I had no idea why the walls glowed, but was grateful for the light. We moved further along through what I thought of, as the wormhole, which gradually started to slant downward.

Progressing further along a slight whisper of sound reached my ears. I paused and listened. The sound of a stringed instrument came from far ahead. What could it be? Surely, we were alone. As we moved further along toward the sound, it changed its tone. Many other sounds joined with the first. The more we hurried on toward the source the louder it became. Then several large drops of water hit me, I knew then the sound was not that of music.

The orchestra which it seemed I had been hearing had changed suddenly becoming a discordant, cacophonous roar of the mighty river Weettan. I could only think, just a few feet of wet earth, was all that separated us from the waters rushing above our heads.

The ceiling dripped even more water the further downward we went. The water around our feet began to rise. Our clothes were soon dripping, and the wetter we became the more anxious I was becoming. We hurried on even faster. The seeping water began to fill the tunnel. The water reached up to our ankles, and then still rising, to our knees, then quickly it became waist deep. I prayed we would make it out before the river collapsed the tunnel, and the water came rushing in. If that happened, we surely would be drowned.

The downward slope of the wormhole changed, becoming more level, and gradually it started upward, hopefully to fresh air and blue sky. We led the animals through the belly deep water as fast as they would move. They needed little urging, they were as eager to escape as we were. We waded and splashed our way forward up the slope of the wormhole.

The water became less deep, receding back to our knees, then to our ankles. The roar of the river faded behind us, becoming more distant. We rushed up the tunnel and out of the water. We had made it to the far side of the mighty Weettan. A feeling of relief washed over me, but it didn't last. Now we needed to find a way out onto dry land.

If the tunnel filled with water, there was still a possibility we would drown. I looked for an opening from which we could escape. There was not an opening I could see. Then I remembered the pick I had bought. Pulling it from the pack on the mule, I yelled at Tagg, "See if you can find a thin spot in the wall. If we are lucky and quick enough, maybe I can bust our way through with the pick."

Tagg had run ahead several feet when he yelled. "Over here, I think I found a spot."

The water was rising again. I hurriedly waded over and looked to where Tagg pointed. Light filtered through a small spot, it did look thin. I swung the pick hard at the stone. It made a small hole. I swung again, harder, and the hole became larger as the pick plunged again and again through the wall. Swinging the pick a huge chunk fell away making the opening larger. Instantly I felt a rush of air going out through the hole. Over the outward rush of air, I heard the roar of the river, coming up the wormhole behind us.

Fear gave me strength, for I did not relish drowning, and worse, I felt responsible for young Tagg, who had hardly started his life's journey. Blow after blow, after blow, I swung the pick furiously in desperation; I was a mad man, about to die. Large chunks of the wall began to fall away. The opening grew larger and larger as I angrily hacked away, but still, it was not large enough to get our nervous animals through.

Then the water started to rise rapidly, reaching past our ankles. I increased the blows with my pick. I became frantic with desperation. I didn't want to die. Suddenly the wall shuddered, gave way, and collapsed leaving an opening large enough for the horse and mule.

I made Tagg go first. Once through the mule ran ahead, with Tagg hanging onto the rope, trying to keep up. I was close on their heels with the stallion.

The rushing waters filled the tunnel as it swept past the opening. It roared on down the wormhole until it could hold no more, and with a loud explosive gush, it blasted forth, out through the opening we had made. We had narrowly escaped with our lives, with no time to spare.

We had hurried as far away from the tunnel as fast as we could. With a great groan, the giant wormhole exploded. Lucky for us we were far enough away, that only a shower of water drenched us. Even though we were soaked, it sure beat the hell out of drowning.

We moved on up a hillock, which rose above the flooded plain. Three lone oak trees stood on the small knoll. We looked back at the swiftly moving river, from which we had narrowly escaped. While building a fire to dry us, Tagg bent over gagged and vomited. "I thought the earth shaking was bad—but water is worse, he said, coughing. What's next, fire?"

"Let us hope not. Well at least we are alive and now on the other side of the river." Then I glanced at the oaks and noticed the grass growing there. "Tagg, after all the excitement we've had today I think we should make camp here. There is grass for the animals among the oaks. We can decide while we rest, our next step." I looked at the far mountains and wondered *what next? Did one of them hold the sought-after treasure?*

Chapter 7

an Old Man

Morning brought a warm breeze and bright sunshine. My contented feeling quickly came and went, as I slapped at the flying insects, biting on any exposed parts of skin, and the crawling ants. At least I didn't see any giant worms. I looked forward to leaving this river and its tormenting bugs far behind. The river had caused us enough trouble. Now my thoughts were on the mountains and reaching them soon.

On day three, we came to the foot of the nearest of five mountains. It was mostly boulders and rocks. Plant life was scarce. I didn't think it was the mountain for which I looked, but being an explorer, one shouldn't pass up any opportunity. I wanted to see what secrets, if any, it might hold. You never know what you might find.

Some distance up the mountainside, we stumbled across a cave. There were many markings of it having already been explored. We found an empty flagon and a broken shovel. We entered through a small opening, and I stooped over, and traveled twenty paces to its end. Nothing.

We searched further on this mountain, finding only one other cave, if you could call it that. Without entering, we could see it ended after a short distance. Not discouraged we left that mountain and headed for the next closest one, which sat a quarter days ride away. It also had nothing to offer, and the mountain after was no better.

The next day, having explored three mountains out of five, we came to what I called the second of the so-called Three Sisters. Zanaturas was a much larger pile of dirt than the others reaching far up into the sky. I had great hopes for this one.

This mountain held more diggings and caves. It would take time to explore them all. Still, we might have luck and find what I searched so desperately for. After exploring the many caves this mountain had to offer, we came up empty handed. I still had not found the treasure cave,

The smallest mountain of the Three Sisters was called Kalamadie. It stood next in line. After two hours of futile exploring, I said. "Tagg, this mountain has nothing to offer. Shall we try our luck on the last of 'The Three Sisters,' the one they call Zantarre?"

Tagg gave a shrug. "Alaric, we go in one dirty cave and find nothing, and then go in another dirty cave and find nothing, again. If this is what exploring is about, I would rather do something else."

"Tagg, you need to have patience if you are to succeed as an explorer, and finding treasure is not always easy. I know it's not exciting for you, but when the rewards come you will then see it was worth all the effort."

~ ~ ~

We explored cave after cave on Zantarre, but found no clues to show us the way. Soon we found ourselves high up the mountainside, which was devoid of most plant life or for that matter any other life on this mountain.

On the second day, after exploring several smaller caves, we were within several rods of getting to the peak of Zantarre. Like Tagg, I started having doubts. Maybe I had been too optimistic about finding the Crystal Cave.

It was afternoon when we discovered another cave. We'd almost missed it, the opening was partially blocked by two, tall large boulders, that had fallen together. They looked like two clasped hands in prayer. I took it to be a good omen.

Where the boulders met the earth, we could see a small opening between them. We squatted down and looked. Tagg said, "I think I can make it through, want me to try."

On his stomach, he crawled and wiggled, into the crevice. There was barely enough room for him, but somehow he managed to squeezed through. Kicking his heels, he disappeared from view.

I waited a moment, and then called out, "What do you see?" He didn't answer. Had he run into trouble? Anxiously I went down on my hands and knees, stuck my head into the small opening, and called again. A faint answer reached my ears.

"It's dark, but I can see a little from the light coming under the bolder, but I can't see far or tell how big the cave is."

"Hold on. I'm going to make the opening big enough for me to get through." I grabbed a shovel and started digging the dirt out from between the boulders. The sun was hot. It beat down mercilessly. Its heat reflecting from the boulders didn't help. By the time the hole was large enough I was dripping with sweat. I passed the shovel and a lantern through to Tagg. Then I crawled, and clawed my way through the tight opening.

I brushed the dirt from my pants with a couple of slaps of my dirty hat. After the heat outside, the cool dampness of the cave was a welcomed relief.

Letting my eyes adjust to the darkness and catching my breath, I lit the lantern. Holding it high I looked down the long sloping floor of the cave. It appeared to be a long tunnel. It went further than I could see from the weak light cast from the lantern. We started along the downward sloping floor, our expectations high.

The tunnel took a slight turn and the small amount of light that filtered through from outside disappeared. Now it was just the two of us, a shovel, and the feeble glow of our lantern. The silence was deafening. The further we progressed into the mountain the lower our banter became, until it seemed we were communicating in whispers.

An eerie sound came from out of the darkness ahead. So slight, a whisper perhaps, or a sigh for help, or *was it the wind coming through the tunnel making such a noise?*

"Tagg, did you hear that?" I said.

He stopped in his tracks and listened. "I heard something. It frightened me," he said. "What was it you think?" He asked.

I held a finger to my lips for silence, "Listen."

Straining to listen, we heard only the moaning of the wind. Then a sound came which was not the wind.

The hair on Tagg's neck stood on end and a shiver ran down his back.

"What was that?" he whispered.

"It didn't sound human whatever it was." I said, drawing my knife. Tagg drew his knife too, and said he was ready.

"Let us see if we can find the source." I said, moving deeper into the tunnel, the lantern showing us the way. We came to where the tunnel suddenly branched off, going into two different directions. We stopped at the junction, trying to decide which to follow. We stood there, listening for the mystifying sound.

A murmur so faint reached our ears. A scratching sound, followed by a rasping noise, and a soft gurgle, came out of the tunnel on our left.

Holding the light high, we moved slowly forward, our knives at the ready. The tunnel took a sharp bend to the left. Rounding the curve, I stopped abruptly and Tagg following so close, bumped into me. "What is it?" he asked, trying to see around me.

"The tunnel has partially collapsed." I answered. "Wait, I think someone is caught." Rushing forward I discovered an old man half buried in the dirt. His skin drawn so tight across his bones, he looked ancient. Shriveled and dying, he lay there crushed by a huge boulder that had fallen from the ceiling. He was beyond our help, so I tried my best to comfort him. I gave him some water. Coughing and choking he looked up with gratitude in his eyes. Eyes that burned with little fire left in them, and which held no hope.

There was not much time left for him, he knew he was dying. For the kindness, I had shown, and with precious few breaths remaining, he gasped out his story. A story so weird and unbelievable, had he not been dying, I would not have believed a word.

In those last few moments, he remembered the boulder had fallen, crushing him against the cave wall. How many days had it been since the cave roof collapsed, he didn't remember. He had lost track of time in the dark. He could not remember, two, three days, a week, maybe longer. He lay there gasping for air, his chest crushed. A cracked rib had probably punctured a lung. Suffering from the pain, he laid there in the dark hardly breathing, remembering.

~ ~ ~

He told us his story as he faded in and out of consciousness. Sometimes his thoughts rambled on incoherently. *Just when untold wealth lay within his grasp, how could this have happened to him? He wondered why fate was so cruel.*

He had been exploring, looking for the Crystal cave. A cave somewhere on a nameless mountain holding untold wealth that only awaited the finder. He had searched many caves which had led him to this particular one. He had a feeling about this one; he could feel it in his bones.

He had hurried down a sloping passageway deeper into the mountain. Rounding a bend, he saw a faint glow ahead. Upon reaching the faint light, he stepped out into a large cavern. His senses left him as he gazed in wonder. The cavern was lit with hundreds of glowing crystals of every shape and color. One caught his eye and he reached down and picked it up.

At that instant, he heard an ominous grinding sound. He turned and looked up to see a giant boulder start to roll across the passageway closing the opening. he panicked and rushed madly for the gap, not wanting to be buried alive, He barely made it, as the stone closed behind him with hardly a sound. Try as he might he could not dislodge it to get back into the treasure cave.

Then he went on, his voice raspy, and gasping for air, whispered, "There is a cave in... in the side of the mountain called Trisha," ...he gasped for air... "some call it Zantarre... having large boulders and... and rocks everywhere. There is a giant boulder sha ,,, shaped like a giant hand." Frothy blood dribbled from a corner of his mouth as he tried to speak.

"There lies an opening... so small" ...he wheezed, "only a small boy... or"... he coughed, spiting up a small amount blood. "or... some one... with great determination might squeeze through. Beware, for there are dangers... in this cave."

"What dangers?" I asked. He had just described the cave we were in, but was it this cave I muse. He rambled so incoherently it was hard to tell if he spoke of this cave, or maybe another.

Coughing and spitting blood, he mumbled, "Beware... the--eyes... bewa... ey-ss."

His pain must have been unbearable. Then he lost consciousness, his rasping breath stopped, and his eyes rolled back showing white. His clenched fist slowly relaxed and his hand fell open. There in his palm lay a plum-sized stone, which radiated yellow fire, even in the dim light cast by the lantern

Had he been coming from the Crystal Cave I wonder, or had he been trying to find another way back in. With all of his ramblings, he had not said.

Chapter 8

the Crystal Cave

Leaving the old man, Tagg and I continued our downward journey along the tunnel, which seemed to go on forever. We came to another place where the passageway was connected to another opening, which headed off in a different direction.

Again, we must make a decision. The tunnel we had been following appeared to be somewhat larger, and this was the one I chose. If I was wrong, we could always come back and explore the other branch.

I felt the air move across my face as the tunnel made another of its unending bends. We could hardly see ten steps into the dark of the damp tunnel. Remembering the old man's dying words, we pushed on slowly and warily not knowing what lay ahead in the darkness.

With my lantern held high to show the way, a cold draft suddenly made the lantern flame flutter. A chill ran through my body as we continued our progress downward. It seemed into the darkness of hell. My hands became clammy. We continued cautiously along the ever-sloping floor into a smaller cavern that ran on for some distance. I must have counted ten bends if I hadn't lost track, from where we had left the old man. I had almost lost patients.

We stumbled ever downward in the dark of the tunnel. Wait, was there a faint glow coming from further ahead, or was my mind starting to see things. Did I rally see a dim glow? I said, "Tagg, you see anything? His younger eyes were much better in the dimly lit tunnel, than were mine.

We stopped and he looked ahead. Then he said, "I think I see something, a dim glimmer maybe, but I'm not sure." Continuing on, we found the light to be reflected off of several large granite boulders, which partially protruded from the cavern walls. The light was coming from around yet another bend. The glow became noticeably brighter, as we approached.

It took only a moment to reach the source. The light filtered out from around the edges of a huge disk-shaped boulder, which effectively blocked the tunnel and our progress. This must be the stone the old man had mentioned. It seemed to have been rolled out from a slot carved in the tunnel wall. I had nothing with which to pry an opening for us to squeeze through.

Tagg trying to get his arm past the boulder exclaimed, "Alaric I feel round holes in the wall. What are they?"

I felt along where his hand was and felt several indentations. "Ah, ha!" I exclaimed, and then I wondered were they man made. I started reaching into all the holes searching for something that would release the boulder, or in someway make it move. Sticking my arm deep into an opening, I felt something, a lever maybe. I couldn't tell which in the dark. "Stand back Tagg, I found a lever, and I'm going to pull it. I don't know what might happen, so be prepared to run."

After a moment, Tagg said, "I don't see anything happening. Alaric did you pull it?"

"Yes, I'm pulling it as hard as I can." I gave the lever several hard jerks. "The lever is moving Tagg, but nothing is happening. Maybe it's a fake. Feel around for another lever." We stuck our hands and arms in every hole we could find. There was no lever.

"There must be a way to move this giant stone. Tagg, feel around on the opposite wall and see if there are other holes over there, and I will keep looking on this side."

"I don't feel any holes." his small voice called out from the other side. "Oh wait, I feel something, it's a hole."

"Is there a lever?"

"No."

"Keep looking, there must be something."

"Wait, here's another hole" Tagg reached into the opening. "Alaric I found it, another lever." he said excitedly.

"Stay there I'm coming." I reached into the opening, felt the lever, and told Tagg to get ready to run. I pulled the lever. Nothing happened. I pulled harder, still nothing. I thought a moment. Then I said, "Maybe if we pull both levers at the same tine, the boulder will move. Tagg, you take this lever, I will take the one on the other side. When I say pull, we both pull the handles. Get ready, okay, pull" At first, nothing happened. Then a low rumble shook the ground and with a scraping noise, the huge boulder slowly rumbled aside.

We rushed forward past the boulder and traveling only a short distance, we rounded another bend and suddenly burst forth into a much larger cavern and stopped dead. Before us was an enormous cavern whose ceiling rose high over our heads.

I rubbed my eyes and took another look. Before us, the Crystal Cave lay gloriously exposed in all its magnificence. We stood gazing in astonishment upon a sight of such splendor and riches, as one had never seen. I felt faint. Almost collapsing in disbelief, I reached out and touching the wall, I steadied myself. I could not believe my good fortune. After searching for years, I had finally found the Crystal Cave.

Tagg and I tentatively stepped forward into the huge cavern, our eyes dazzled from the light, as bright as day, cast from the many massive crystals that grew haphazardly in a disorganized mess of confusion. Sprouting from the floor, they tilted in many different directions. Some must be twenty feet long or longer, with three feet across each of their many sides.

Scattered among the crystal columns were large gemstones of every color and hue. There were blue, red, yellow, and green stones of every size. *They must be priceless*, I thought. It was a sight unlike any I had ever seen. Tagg started forward, and I held an arm out to stop him. "Let's not be too hasty, danger may dwell here."

Tag's eyes were wide and his mouth hung open. "Alaric, what is this? I... I have never seen... what are those things coming out of the floor?" He stuttered.

"They appear to be giant crystals, and I have never seen anything like it, not even in all my travels. They surely are a wondrous sight to behold aren't they?" In awe, we stood mesmerized by the grandeur of the enormous jungle of opaque crystals that seemed a jumble mess. As I studied the crystals, it seemed that most of them leaned or tilted in the same direction, as if they were pointing. *It made me wonder.*

I took a tentative step forward. Nothing happened. Emboldened I took another. Still nothing occurred. I stood there thinking. Suddenly Tagg stepped past me. I yelled, "Tagg, stop." I reached for him, and missed.

Tagg ran through the nearby crystals, his arms spread wide, laughing and touching them with his fingertips. A glittering red jewel, as large as my hand caught his eye, and he bent to pick it up. I yelled again, "Tagg don't touch it." He paid no heed to my warning and picking up the red orb, he turned to me holding it high, his arm outstretched and laughing.

He was still laughing as he turned into a small five-foot crystal with a red tip. Unnerved, I stumbled back and half-collapsing, I sat down hard on the cave floor, stunned. Tagg—was gone.

I sat there for quite some time, staring at the crystal that held Tagg, hoping this was a dream, or maybe only temporary. I sat not moving, only starring, nothing further occurred. I was afraid to move, and almost in tears, over Tagg. I thought of the old man. How had he missed being turned into a giant crystal?

In the short time, I had known Tagg, he had wormed his way into my heart, and I had come to think of him as a son. Now he was gone. Devastated, I sat there. The tears welled up in my eyes and started running down my cheeks. I brushed them aside, and holding my head between my hands, I wondered why?

Chapter 9

escape From Crystal Cave

How long I sat there staring at the crystals I don't know. Deep in thought, I had lost track of time thinking of Tagg. He had been great company and an asset. If it were not for him, I would not now be in the Crystal Cave. Then gradually I became aware the giant crystals were changing color. Slowly they begin taking on a faint greenish tinge. I stood watching in bewilderment and wonder.

From the corner of my eye, I saw the source of the green light, which in all the excitement had gone unnoticed. A large golden throne on a raised platform of silver sat alone, amidst the jumble of crystals. *How had I failed to notice it?*

A large velvet cushion of royal blue rested upon the throne, and sitting in its center was a glittering green stone as large as my head. Pulsing like a beating heart the stone cast its brilliance of green fire throughout the cave. This was caught and reflected ten-fold from the many crystals, making it almost brighter than the sun. Entranced, I watched as the stone began to glow with more intensity, and the brighter it glowed, the larger it grew. I shaded my eyes, and rooted to the spot watched with wonder, what was occurring.

The green stone had double in size, and then doubled again. It kept growing larger by the moment, until it was almost as large as me, then it stopped. I could only stare. I would never be able to carry such a large stone.

The stone shimmered before my eyes and changed shape. *Was I loosing my eyesight?* I rubbed and blinked my eyes for a moment to clear my vision. When I looked again, the stone was gone and in its place sat the most beautiful woman I had ever seen.

In all of my worldly travels, I had seen my share of beautiful women, but this one made all the others look like milking maids. She glowed with the same radiance, as the green stone, from whence she had been transformed.

Was she real?

I blinked rapidly, closed my eyes tight shut, shook my head and opened my eyes. She was still there. She must be real. Without thinking, I started towards her. She quickly stood, and held her hand palm out, in a gesture for me to stop. I remembered Tagg's fate, almost afraid to take a breath I stood not moving.

~ ~ ~

Once again, I stopped telling my story. Miiliinda had a confused look on her face. She said, "Why didn't you just use your magical powers to overcome the spells?"

"Miiliinda, you must have forgotten. You do remember, at that time I still had no magical powers."

She nodded, "Yes, now I remember." Then she apologized and said, "Your story is so fascinating, I keep forgetting it was in your past. Please do continue. I can hardly wait for you to finish the telling of it."

"Now where was I? Oh yes, I was trapped in the Crystal Cave."

~ ~ ~

My gaze was riveted on her radiant face as I stood motionless. Her lips moved but no sound ensued forth. Her lips moved again without sound. and I felt a very slight tickle in my head. A female voice, as sweet as music, wove itself through my head. It commanded me to move very carefully, and only as she directed, which tweas just fine with me. I didn't want to be turned into a crystal like Tagg.

Then the soft, sweet sounding voice in my head said, "My name is Emerauld. This cavern is a trap. For the many that enter here, most do not leave. Only move as I command or you too may become ensnared. You see,

I cannot move from this throne, unless certain things are done to free me. I also am a prisoner in this grand trap, but with your help, I can be set free, and able to leave this place. I have waited so long for this moment. Now sir, how may I address you?"

"My name is Alaric. Why cannot you just walk out? I see nothing to stop you."

"I am held here against my will by magical spells, cast by my evil sister. You are one of the few not to be turned into a giant crystal and trapped here forever, and I have great hope for you. I am locked in this space by a special key which my sister wears on a gold chain around her neck. You must get the key to release me. It will not be easy, for you see; she is the Queen, Queen Gurgold. She rules Borrgess with a strong hand. If you can set me free and help me to regain the throne, you will be well rewarded, this is my promise to you."

"If I manage to get out of here without being turned into a crystal, how do I get the key?"

"The Queen sleeps in her room away from the King. If you can slip into the Castle unnoticed and find her room, there might be a chance of stealing it from under her nose as she sleeps." She laughed with an infectious, tinkling laugh.

"Alright, guide me out of here and I will do my best to set you free." I said.

"Before you leave there is something I must give to you." She said. "It may help in your retrieval of the key"

She gave me directions for the moves I should make, but they didn't take me out of the cavern. I ended standing next to the golden throne, and its most wondrous lady, who was even more beautiful close up than I had previously thought. She reached out and taking my hand pulled me closer. I wondered how she could do this if she could not leave the throne.

She explained. "Do you see this beautiful gold necklace, which I wear around my neck? It was placed there by my sister. It holds the magic that keeps me bound to this throne. Take special notice of the fastener on the necklace. The small opening you see is for a very small key. Once the necklace is unlocked and opened, the spell will be broken and I shall be free.

That is why you must get the key."

All the while, she talked, I edged closer. Unable to control myself, I Suddenly reached out and pulled her close against me. Holding her face between my hands, I pressed my lips gently to hers and she trembled slightly. It must have been a long time between kisses for her, for she pressed her warm body tightly against mine and kissed me feverishly, and with such passion, which I had never encountered before.

With that kiss, and at that moment, I fell in love. With that kiss, she gave me more than her passion; she gave me a small part of her magical powers....

Then she told me a story, of her carefree life as a royal child. Of the abusive sister, her fraternal twin, that most of the time had been impulsive and unpredictable.

After the telling of her story, she warned me once again, not to touch anything in the cavern. Not all but most of the glittering stones scattered among the crystal columns contained a spell. That if touched would encase one in a large crystal. I remembered Tagg's fate.

With that warning, I stepped most carefully between the giant crystals, following her directions as she guided me to the cavern's opening. I glanced quickly at some of the giant crystal columns, and grimaced. Most contained a man. My steps became even more careful on my way to freedom.

Stepping past the large rolling stone entrance, I took a deep breath and looked back at Tagg one last time. Then I turned and hurried out from this forbidden place as fast as my legs would carry me.

"That is my story Miiliinda, and so here we are."

"And what did this Emerauld, that you fell in love with, after just one kiss, tell you?" I asked rather harshly. My eyes misted over, my shoulders sagged. I was devastated by his words. Cast aside was any faint beginnings of falling in love with this stranger called Alaric... Now that dream was shattered. Crestfallen, I looked down at the white wolf at my feet Alaric didn't notice. He was too enthralled in his telling of Emerauld.

He said "Emerauld told me a story of her and her sister growing up, which was so fantastic and unbelievable, it had to be true. Would you care to hear it? It should not take me long to retell."

He didn't see the tear she wiped from her eye. She sighed, and said, "Please do, if you must."

"Alright then," he said with enthusiasm, "I will tell you the story as Emerauld told it to me, in her own her words."

Chapter 10

the Sisters

E[illegible]*gave, then retold to Miiliinda.*

[illegible]

[illegible]

Several years earlier...

I was the first-born, by a minute or so. My sister followed shortly thereafter, screaming and kicking. My mother, who was Queen Fen-Milar, took us both from the midwife, one in each arm to her breast and suckled us. My sister stopped screaming, her mouth full of warm milk.

This was a precursor of the years that were soon to follow.

As princesses, we had everything we wanted, bestowed upon us by our loving and caring parents. Nothing was too good for us. I wanted very little, but my spoiled sister Gurgold, would cry and throw tantrums, until she got what she wanted, and she wanted everything. Which mother and father almost always gave to her.

Need I say, she was for much of the time, only concerned with herself, and what she could finagle? Most of **5 7** the time, as long as she got her way, we had fun together, doing things that young girls do. There was a time growing up when we were as inseparable as two peas in a pod. Once we took our stallions for a ride, after the stable boy had saddled them. We were ten years of age at the time. I remember that spring well, the flowers were blooming and the trees were leafing. It was beautiful, my favorite time of the year.

Our father, King Vaarzen, was renown in the kingdom as a great horseman. He could do things with a horse that others only dream of doing. His father had started him riding before he could even walk, he had told us. Therefore, you could say he was most knowledgeable when it came to riding.

We were barely able to walk when our father, the king, had put us on ponies, against mothers' protestations. Neither of us fell off, to the delight of father. Not having a son to carry on his name he had raised and treated us as he would have, if we had been sons. We never thought of ourselves as ladies, we were tomboys and as such had many adventures.

Sometimes we got into trouble with someone, or something and had to answer to father. With fathers training and a few astute suggestions, it was inevitable that we soon had outgrown the ponies. We wanted a horse that was taller, stronger, and faster. Thus, for us it could only be a stallion. Mother fought and argued, but father won as he almost always did.

That day, we had ridden out of the courtyard into the countryside. My dark haired sister and I talked, discussing what to do as we passed over a slight hill and out of sight of the castle. We rode slowly, our horses' close, while we chatted. We let the horses pick the way, weaving in and out around the large oaks, which grew on the grassy sloping hillside that curved gently down to the slow flowing river.

My sister Gur,' we never used our full names when alone, had started arguing that she was bored riding over the same places day after day. She wanted to explore somewhere new. She said, "Em' the river is so low, let's cross and see what's on the other side. Father will never know."

With all of her pleading, I finally gave in and with a toss of my long golden locks said, "Alright, but we shouldn't go to far from the river we could become lost and you know how father gets when he's mad."

The river, Grazalor, was low for this time of year and we easily crossed to the other side without mishap, the water not even reaching to the horse's knees. We had never been this far from the castle before. For some unknown reason, father had warned us not to go beyond the river.

After riding awhile, we sighted a small green valley. At its far end lay a small rounded mountain. Gur' headed in that direction with me trailing.

Riding through the valley, Gur' suddenly said, "Em,' I going to ride over to that little mountain. We can go exploring, it would be an adventure and fun, don't you agree?"

"I think we should go back." I answered. "We are going to be in a lot of trouble if anyone finds out we disobeyed father."

"I don't care if he does find out. I'm tired of being treated like a child, anyway." She complained.

"Well we are only ten. I would say I am still just a young lady. But, Gur', I'm not sure about you." I said as she galloped off, heading towards the small mountain, my words trailing after her. I kicked my heels at the stallion's side and he took off like the wind after Gur'. By the time I caught her we were almost to the mountain. Close up, it was more of a large hill than a mountain. Trees spotted its rounded sides in a random pattern.

Gur' started up its side, stopping at the top. I pulled up alongside and looked out over the landscape. "Gur' look I can see the castle from here."

She was looking the other way down the hill where several boulders had crashed down from higher up opening a huge gash in doing so. She wanted to explore the gash. When we reached it, we could see where the falling boulders had opened an entrance to a cave, from which a strong musty odor emanated. The cave appeared to be very old. It must have been sealed for a very long, long, time. The pungent odor which assailed my nose was foul, like something had died.

Gur' became excited on our discovery. She quickly jumped down from her horse and tying it to a bush, she looked up at me, and said "Let's see what's here shall we?" Without waiting for an answer, she darted into the dark forbidding opening.

I yelled, "Gur', wait for me," as I hurried to catch up. The stench was so strong, we tied our silk scarves from around our necks, across our nose, and then we stepped further into the darkness. "Gur', we shouldn't be doing this lets go back."

"Yes. Maybe you're right it is to dark for exploring."

I was glad that she had agreed with me for a change. My hopes shot up, and just as fast they were immediately shattered, when she said, "Wait Em', I think I see a light farther on." I went further inside the cave opening and stood beside Gur' and stared hard down the tunnel. Of course, my sister was right. She is always right as far as she is concerned. Straining my eyes, I thought I could see a faint glimmer of light in the far distance. It didn't seem much of a light, only a very faint glow.

My sister said, "Shall we. Let's see what it's about?" Off she went without my answer leaving me alone in the dark. I hurried and caught up. Trying my best to talk her out of going any further into the dark hole, but it was like talking to a stonewall. She kept right on walking and the glow was becoming brighter and brighter. I looked back, all I could see was a small pinpoint of light that was the cave opening. We were far to deep into this hill it seemed to me. It was eerily quiet, and I was somewhat afraid. But Gur" she just trudged on toward the glow.

At last, we arrived at the source. The walls of the tunnel were actually glowing, casting an eerie light that reflected not even our shadows. In the dull glow, we saw that the tunnel split into two directions. I looked at Gur'. Even though she was younger than me, but only by a minute, I was the one that led most of the time. This time it was different, it was her adventure so I waited for her to speak.

Em', you take the tunnel on the right and I'll take the other one. If you don't find anything, meet me back here. There was no use to argue with her, I could see she had her stubborn mind made up. So hesitantly, I stepped past the glowing entrance into the darkness. I had taken maybe a hundred steps, maybe more, I didn't count. Then in the black darkness, I felt something had brushed by me and then swirled on past into the tunnel. Suddenly the walls started glowing with a bright silver luminosity. Ahead I could see a swirling film of pure white. It stopped swirling and there in its midst floated a beautiful woman dressed in a gown of pure white, glittering, finery.

I became frightened. She looked into my eyes and I into hers, I could hear her words in my head. "Be not frightened little one, nor afraid, for I will not harm you. She swirled around me; I was embraced with such a warm, good feeling, that wasn't warm at all, but rather cool. I was feeling so good, I felt like I was floating. Then I looked down and almost fainted, for I was floating, as high as the *Lady in white.*

Even though her lips did not move, she spoke to me. I could hear her words. "I am the queen lady of all goodness, and my child, I can see that you are pure of heart. Therefore, I will endow you with certain powers, which you will not understand immediately. However, over the years and given time, you will come to understand what they are and how to use them. When that time happens and you become twenty years of age they will be wholly yours." Then she gave a warning, "But these powers are only to be used for good."

I opened my mouth to speak. The white light of the lady expanded ever brighter, and brighter, until, it became so bright I closed my eyes against its brilliance. When I opened them, the lady was gone, and once again, I stood on the dirt floor of the tunnel.

Dazed and Stunned for the moment, I must have hallucinated. *Was it from the odor or maybe the fumes,* I wondered. If what the lady said were true, I didn't feel any different. It must not have really happened.

I had lost all track of time. I looked down the tunnel for the pinprick of light to guide me. Then I noticed that I could see the walls in the dark. I looked down at my body. My arms, hands, legs and feet were glowing, casting a dim radiance about me. Something *had* happened to me.

Now that I could see, I hurried to meet my sister where the tunnel had split. She was not there. I waited awhile for her and then started thinking. Should I go down the other tunnel and try to find her, she might be in trouble. Then I heard a sound coming from the tunnel and looked up to see my sister stager forth, from the opening. It was not the sister that I knew. Her haughtiness' was gone. There were dark circles around her eyes. She looked as if she hadn't slept in a week. Her clothes were in disarray. She appeared dazed like she was lost.

My mouth working, I finally got out, "Gur', what happened to you? You look terrible."

She leaned unsteadily against the opening, while gasping for breath. She couldn't answer. It was then I noticed a pure white streak running through her black hair. it had not been there before. I gasped and reached out to touch the streak. "Don't touch me!" She spouted venomously in anger.

My sister had always been head strong and sometimes violent, but I had never seen her like she was now. She radiated unfriendliness, in an utterly, intensely, cruel demeanor.

"Gur', I started..."

She cut me off abruptly. "Don't ever call me Gur again. My name is Gurgold."

"But Gur'..." Her eyes flashed red and she stalked off toward the pinpoint of light. From that moment on, we were split apart like an apple that had been halved. No longer were we best friends or for that matter, sisters.

~ ~ ~

Ten hears later...

Over the years, Gur had turned ever more hateful and repulsive looking. Father couldn't handle her, and I believed she was the cause of my Mothers early death, from unknown causes. There were whispers among the servants in the castle that Gurold my sister had caused it. Suspicions were cast, but nothing proved.

Then two years later, we were dinning one evening, when father suddenly clutched his chest and collapsed in his chair, his eyes open wide, staring... directly at Gurgold.

I rushed to his side. "Father what is it?" I screamed, to no avail. Father was dead.

Gurgold showed no emotion, but her eyes crinkled ever so slightly with a faint upward curve of her lips. I thought.

Couriers were sent on horseback to all the royalty, throughout the surrounding countryside, with word of my father, King Vaarzens death. Kings, Queens, Princes and Princesses that my father had respected were invited to his burial.

Three days later father was interred in the family's stone burial chamber.

We held a banquet in the Hall of Kings, to show our appreciation of all who had attended the burial service. I let Gurgold handle all the arrangements, since I was in tears for most of the time, grieving for my father whom I most dearly loved. The long tables in the hall would seat fifty people and all had been taken. There was many conversations during the banquet, some were loud and some in whispers.

In between dabbing at my eyes, I glanced around at all the gathered nobles. Most of the faces I knew, and all reflected grief. Among the many there were more than a few that also held a worried look, for father was the one that kept the peace between the different kingdoms. He kept them from fighting one another.

Afterwards, being the first-born and when the scepter would be past on to me. I intended to give a short speech of appreciation, thanking everyone who had attended the service.

My eyes wandered about over the crowd. Then for some reason, I looked at the servers who stood quietly back against the ornate wall tapestry, waiting attentively upon the needs of each guest. One server for each guest was stationed behind. Curiously, I wondered why beside each server stood an Elite Guardsman. It was unusual to say the very least. However, Gurgold had arranged everything. So I thought no more about it in my grieving until...

As I stood getting everyone's attention and ready to speak, I was suddenly surrounded by four of the Kings Elite Guardsmen and placed under arrest. Several of the guest stood immediately voicing their anger, demanding to know the reason for such actions. They stood awaiting an answer, unsure of what to expect, but fearing something untoward was about to occur.

Gurgold stood as the guards swiftly removed me from the hall. She then quieted the disturbed guest. Speaking quickly, she then announced to all, that she was accepting the sce.pter, and now would be the reining Queen. She would be taking the place of King Vaarzen. Even though Emerauld should be queen, she was unfit to rule, so the kingdom falls to me.

Several of the Kings present stood to object. Some started yelling that was not protocol that the scepter was always passed to the oldest heir. At this outburst, several uniformed guardsmen at Gurgold's signal, stepped quickly forward and stood directly behind all the dissenters, who suddenly stopped their yelling and looked about in fear. For there were many guardsmen present in the great hall, and they were well prepared to quell any dissenters. A great silence swept quickly over the crowd.

In one moment, my sister had usurped my power. I was escorted to the library and locked in, with two guardsmen stationed outside the doors. Furious and angry, I strode back and forth, crossing the room from the locked door to window and looked out, then back I went to the door, several times, thinking and fuming all the while.

There came a scrape of a key in the lock, and the door swung opened. There stood my sister with hate in her eyes and a small, tight smile, twisted on her lips. "Gurgold, are you out of your mind? Have you gone completely mad, or crazy? What has happened to you that you dare treat me this way?"

"It's what you deserve. Oh, you're so pure, always looking down on me and my ways. Now look at you, your not so high and mighty now." She laughed. "Now I have all the power. I will tell you a secret. I have power you couldn't dream of. A power that was given me in that cave we explored some years back." She took a step forward, and looking me in the face, said. "You do remember that time, don't you?"

"Yes," I said, staring into her cold eyes. "I do remember, and you are not the sister I went into the cave with." I turned quickly, brushed a tear away and went to the window and looking out across the green countryside I said, "what happened to my sister Gur'?" Then turning around I stepped forward, awaiting her answer.

"Emerauld, that sister is no more and since you abhor me, I am putting you where you cannot stop me from doing whatever I want." She uttered a command, "Guards bind her hands and get the carriage ready we're taking a short trip." She held up her hand, "No! Wait! On second thought, saddle the stallions. I will take her riding just her and me alone."

"She then brought me to this mountain called Zantarre, and with her black magic, created this Crystal Cave with a throne, and all that you see here. This will be your kingdom, she told me. However to keep me from using my own magic, she placed this gold necklace, which nullifies my powers, around my throat and locked it in place,"

~ ~ ~

Alaric spread his arms in a helplessly gesture, and said, "So Miiliinda, Emerauld still waits there for me. I must somehow get the key that will unlock her necklace, and release her from the spell, that has been cast upon her. So little one you see... Oh, forgive me. I know you hate being call little one.

Miiliinda, I have been here many days and nights waiting for your arrival. I hope with your powers and mine combined, we can set her free. Will you help?"

Miiliinda looked down at the white wolf that lay contented at her feet.

Chapter 11

the Wolf ~ my Brother

While he waited for her answer, Alaric said, "Miiliinda I can see you must have many questions about the wolf. Let me explain, why I call this wolf my brother. I can see in your inquisitive eyes that you are more than curious."

She looked up with a weak smile and said, "Alright, explain."

After I left Emerauld, I sent for Raddick. He wasn't a wolf at that time, only my younger brother. Thinking he might help in stealing the key, that hung on a chain around the fat neck of the Queen.

We met a fortnight later on a side street in Borrgess, at a small eating-place. As we sat eating, we discussed the problems of obtaining the key. The easiest way would be to kill her, but then we would be caught and in all likelihood hung. I could use the magic powers given me by Emerauld, but I was neither adept nor confident enough to use them.

My brother said we could masquerade as highwaymen. When the queen takes her ride in the evening, riding around the countryside, as she often did in her carriage, we would intercept her. Wearing masks, we could stage a holdup and take all of her jewels and also the necklace with the key. We thought the plan worthy, so therefore we decided to give it a try. We could always escape on our horses if the plan failed, or so we thought.

We stopped the carriage one evening at sunset, just moments before the sun passed below the horizon. The shadows were long. We wore our hats pulled low. I held a pistol, while Raddick stepped down from his horse and moved forward to take the Queen's jewelry. We figured on disappearing in the ensuing darkness.

"Your jewels, or your life my queen," I spoke from behind the mask as Raddick approached the carriage holding an open bag.

She took one look at us and laughed. "You low-caste scum... I am the Queen. Why do you bother me? Be gone, before I loose my wrath upon you."

She surely was not in any fear of us. I said, "Go on my brother, collect her jewels and don't forget that pretty necklace, around her neck."

Raddick stepped forward toward the Queen. "That's when she pointed her finger at him, uttered several words, of which I didn't understand, and poof. My brother was transformed into the white wolf that now lies at your feet. Upon seeing a wolf suddenly appear my horse bolted, it was all I could do to stay on him. By the time I got control, the carriage was long gone, but my brother the wolf, was still with us and alive."

"At first, he enjoyed being a wolf and the freedom of running wild. Between that foiled robbery and now, I have tried using some of the magical powers given me by Emerauld and the more I use them the easier it becomes. Raddick and I communicate by thought."

"However, he yearns to once again be in human form, since he set eyes on you, that stormy night when you arrived. I have tried using some of the magic Emerauld gave me; to undue, the queens spell and free Raddick. But alas, as you can see, Raddick is still trapped in the form of a wolf."

"Yes I do see," Replied Miiliinda. Running her fingers affectionately across the long fur of the wolf,

"Raddick is a very handsome wolf, I must say." Her eyes glittered as she stroked the wolf, then she smiled to herself, *a very handsome wolf Indeed.*

"Alaric, how do you now purpose to get the key from around the queen's neck?"

"Well, after dark, and after the queen has gone to bed, we could sneak into the castle, slip into the Queen's Chambers, and somehow steal it from around her throat." He paused. "I really don't know, but there has to be a way." He said, frustrated.

"And just how do you plan on getting past the guards and into the castle."

Alaric sat on the grass next to Miiliinda and Raddick. Putting his head in his hands he muttered, "I don't know. I just don't know. You have any ideas?"

"First we have to get past the guards into the castle. Then find our way to her room without getting caught, and then get in without making any noise, then get the necklace, and then somehow get out, all without being seen or caught."

Miiliinda said, "Sounds easy."

She sat thinking as did Alaric. "I know, we could wait until she throws a Royal Ball, and slip in, and while you danced with her you could grab the necklace from her neck, and run. No, that's no good you would be caught." She thought some more. "Maybe we could find another way to get in."

"I know," Alaric spoke out, "I just remembered something that Emerauld said. That she and her sister used to sneak out sometimes through an entrance somewhere in back of the castle. If we can find that doorway, it might get us in without being seen."

"We can send Raddick to look for the door. He's so fast no one could ever catch him and who would ever expect a wolf to be looking for a way into the castle." While we made our plans, Raddick slept.

In the dark before the moon rose, the three of us slunk like thieves, through the shrubbery up to the rear of the cold, stone castle, looking for the secret door.

Raddick could move faster, so he led the way forward, with the natural stealth of a wolf to his gait. Quietly we edged close below a towering, rounded moss covered stonewall, of a tall tower, which held several windows. All were dark, except for one solitary window high up, from which light shone forth. Could it be Gurgold's? If it was, was she awake?

While looking up at the open window, I lost track of Raddick in the darkness. "Miiliinda stay close," I whispered. "I've lost sight of Raddick." I felt her hand touch my shoulder. Reaching up I grasped it and slowly moved forward holding it firmly. I didn't want Miiliinda getting separated and lost in the dark, for I couldn't see a thing.

Feeling my way along the moss-covered wall, I had not taken ten steps, when I jerked my hand back and uttered an oath. In the dark, my fingers had touched a dreaded Raven- Thorn vine. With a low screech, it had pierced my fingertip leaving it burning and throbbing in pain." Alaric, what happened?" Miiliinda asked, "Are you alright?"

"No! I haven't much time." I uttered through clenched teeth. "Give me a moment." I took a deep breath. In severe pain, I explained, speaking quickly and rapidly, about the Raven-Thorn vine."

'Full-grown it could become larger than a man. When it reached that size, it would then send out several branching vines a hundred feet in every direction. Some as large around as the arm of a man and spaced every three feet along each vine was a ring of thorns, each shaped like a Ravens head. If one touched the thorns they would screech, and quickly bite, injecting its painful venom. The venom in a short span of time would paralyze whatever had been bitten. As paralyzing took effect all body functions ceased to work, causing death.'

As I explained all of this to Miiliinda, I could feel the numbness creeping up my arm. The bite was fatal. Miiliinda took my hand in hers; touched my throbbing finger, uttered words I didn't understand and the pain and numbness were gone. Miiliinda's magic, had saved me from a painful sure death.

I was very carefully after that, as we cautious made our way past the dangerous Raven-Thorn vine. Once past, I again felt the damp moss covered stones of the wall. Feeling for Miiliinda's hand and squeezing it I said, "Thank you for saving me from the Raven-Thorn." She could not see the gratitude reflected on my smiling face in the darkness.

"I think that must be why I was sent here. To assist in all of your endeavors, and help you win back the kingdom." She whispered softly. "Now let's see if we can find that secret door, if there is one."

At that moment, Raddick came bounding up. I guess he could see better in the dark than either Miiliinda or me. He reached out with his thoughts. He had found a door he thought might be the right one.

Around the curve of the towers wall to the furthermost rear of the castle, he led us and stopped where the curved wall of the tower met a straight wall of the castle. In the dark, it was hard to tell if there was a door or not, it was completely grown over by some kind of ivy. Thank the Gods; it was not Raven-Thorn. From the overgrowth, it must have been years since this door had been used. Finally, we cleared a path to the door.

A lever was located to one side, with which to open it. The lever would not budge. Frozen after years of neglect I thought. Maybe I might jar it loose. I picked up a large stone and quietly pounded it once, twice, thrice and again. The handle moved but the door would not open. I turned to Miiliinda, "Any ideas?"

"Hmm, let me think." she whispered. She brushed past me and tried the door she pushed hard but it didn't budge. "It must be locked... Hmm."

Touching the hard oak, metal-strapped door there was no way we could gain entry without a key. We leaned against the door thinking. Suddenly Miiliinda gave a squeal and jumped away from the door.

"What!... Something, scare you, or did you think of something?" Miiliinda didn't answer, but stood with her mouth open, looking down at her cape. In the dim glow of the rising moon, I saw what had surprised Miiliinda. The pocket of her cape moved, jerking in one direction and then the other, like a trapped animal struggling for freedom. Stunned, I could only stare.

Her mouth opened in surprise and wonder. Then she reached into the pocket of her cape and pulled forth a gold and silver key attached to a short broken silver chain. The Key changed shape as she held it out so Alaric could see.

"Alaric I found this key by the obelisk. It was laying half buried in the dirt. In all this time, I had forgotten about it until just now, when it moved. The key is alive or else it has some magical power that it can change shape. I feel it wants to be with the door. Shall we try it? With its shape changing ability, it just might open the door."

She moved the key forward, when the key touched the lock opening it again changed shape, fitting the opening like a glove. "So it fits." she said with a light laugh of disbelief. She gave the key a turn and the lock clanked open as the iron bolt slid back into the door.

The door had not been used in years, its hinges' rusted with age, screeched as we pulled at it. As we tugged at the old door, a small black snake slithered out through the open crack and silently disappeared in the dim moonlight. Then the door swung open to a small foul smelling musty room. A room which had been shut up for far too long, greeted us. A circular stair led upward in the dark gloom. We entered warily, brushing at the cobwebs. The sound of scurrying rodent's tiny claws, as they scampered across the stone, spoke of long disuse.

Alaric sent Raddick ahead. His animal senses were more acute than a persons and he was much more silent and faster than we could ever be. Up the dark stairwell, the wolf crept silently then disappeared into the darkness.

Not making a sound, we followed quickly upward after Raddick. Staying particularly close to, the towers curving wall up we went. One misstep in climbing the stairs and we should most certainly plunge to our death far below. For there was neither a handrail, nor handhold, to keep either of us from the open space, the stairs curled around.

Feeling our way along the stone of the wall our hands touched wood. A door, smaller than the one by which we had entered. It was locked.

"Miiliinda, try the key, if it worked for one door, might it not work for another?" I could hear her fumble in the dark for the pocket and then the key.

"Alaric, I have the key, give me a moment to find the lock opening." She paused. "Got it, the key is squirming into the opening. Now it's stopped. I'm going to turn it now, are you ready? The lock sprung opened with a dull clunked.

Alaric slowly pushed the door open a crack, then a bit more and peered out into a dimly lit passage way. There were no guardsmen they could see. He whispered, "I don't think this is the Queen's floor. I think she would reside higher up. Somewhere that had a daytime view from the window, don't you think?"

"Yes, of course, you are right; the queen would not live on the ground floor. If I were queen, I would live on the very top floor so I could survey all the countryside and keep watch on the people living there."

He closed the door, and I locked it and dropped the key into my pocket. We were again in the dark stairwell headed upward.

Alaric said, "Miiliinda, I think the light coming from the open window we saw must be the queen's room. Which if I'm not mistaken is still three floors above us."

I was about to agree, when something brush against my leg. I jumped back, lost my balance and was on my way to falling off the stairs edge, when a strong hand grabbed me and pulled me back from the edge. As I regained some of my composure, I realized what I had felt was Raddick. He had returned.

Alaric reached out to Riddick's mind. After a moment Alaric said, "I was right, Riddick told me the Queen is on the top floor. Now all we have to do is figure a way into her room without being discovered, steal the necklace, and get out without anyone seeing us. That should be easy, don't you think Miiliinda?" Then he laughed softly. We stood in the dark thinking.

Chapter 12

a tiny Gold Key ~ a big Black Raven

We continued our upward journey, without a plan of action. We both thought hard as we climbed the stone steps, to what, for what. To save the rightful Queen, and restore her to power for her country, and the people who dwelled beneath her rule. Her rule would be fair and equal among all.

The three of us came at last to a door at the end of the towers stairwell. Without light, it had been a long arduous climb, as we fought our way through one cobweb after another. Until we stood in the dark, breathing hard at what might be our last breath? Trying to avoid the scurrying, squealing rats, we wondered what lay beyond the heavy oak door that barred our way.

I withdrew the key from my cloak. The key squirmed in my hand, while I felt for and found the keyhole. The key quickly changed shape to fit the opening. I inserted the key and asked in a whisper. "Are you ready, Alaric?" I heard the sound of his sword as he unsheathed it.

"Yes, I'm ready. Unlock the door, and Miiliinda, try to be quiet about it."

I turned the key gently in the lock and the bolt slid back noiselessly with only a slight snick. Alaric, sword in hand pushed the door open slightly and peered down an elaborately decorated hallway lit only by the light, reflected from candle lit sconces, which hung on the walls.

Seeing no one, we stepped silently into the carpeted corridor and closed the door behind us. Standing a moment, we listened for any sound. Hearing nothing, Alaric sword in hand led the way toward a closed door far down the long hallway. We move swiftly making no sounds. Upon reaching an ornate door, we decided it must be the queen's chamber, for it was elaborate in its design.

Alaric tried the handle, it turned but the door wouldn't open. "It must be latched from the inside. Probably by a wood bar set in iron brackets." he said. A frown creased Alaric's forehead, and shrugging his shoulders he said, "It appears we'll have to find another way in."

I looked around. To the left of the locked door and against the outside wall, stood a small oak table, with a large vase of roses setting upon it. Directly behind the vase of roses was a small window that looked to be open. "Alaric, maybe we can get to her room through this open window."

To gain access to the window we eased the table further down the wall. Being carful not to let the vase fall, Alaric stuck his head out to have a look. "What do you see?" I whispered, trying to look over his shoulder.

He withdrew from the opening and said. "There's a balcony of sorts running below the window. It has a small table and a chair which sets in front of a very large ornate door. It has to be the queen's chamber, shall we try our luck?" he said, as he squeezed through the tight opening. Once he stood on the balcony, he reached backed to help me through the small window. We walked carefully around the table and chair and moved toward a tall wide door, which at first glance seemed closed. Alaric said "Miiliinda don't make a sound, while I see if the door is locked."

He turned to the door and reached out. Suddenly, from out of the dark and without warning, came the flutter of wings.

Startled Alaric tensed. A large black raven had landed on his arm. Stunned he stared at the bird. He recovered his composure somewhat and calmly said. "Now just where did you come from?" The large black Raven which had landed on his out-stretched arm cocked its head, and peered at him, with a gleaming black-eyed stare. Alaric stood disconcerted.

Then he felt the slightest feather light touch in his mind. Almost like a soft breeze. His senses responded automatically to the touch. He reached out with his mind, as he often did with his brother Raddick, when he wished to converse.

The raven twisted his head and peered at Miiliinda then back at me. A voice in my head echoed in sync with the raven's caw, as his hooked beak opened and closed with the words, "I am Jordaar, the rightful Captain of the Kings-Guard, and *you*, who might you be he cawed?"

I felt like strangling the raven he was so noisy, then I realized the noise was all in my mind. When he spoke, his beak did open, but no sound ensued forth. I quickly explained what Miiliinda and I were about. We were here to save the rightful Queen, from where her sister had imprisoned her.

Jordaar replied he would do anything to get rid of the imposter who had taken the throne by force. And he wished to put the rightful heir on the throne, where she belonged, and of course to regain his human form.

He told how Gurgold had bribed several of the key guards and put the rest into the castles dungeon to rot, because they would not go along with her plans to take the throne. In a fit of spite, she had turned him into a raven. He was ready to help in whatever way he could.

"Okay, let me think of how you might be of help." Alaric explained that we were here to steal a key, which dangled from a necklace around Gurgold's fat neck.

The raven flew from my arm and perched on the back of the chair. Cocking his head, he stared at me, with those beady black eyes of his. Then he laughed and asked what my plan was. "I have no plan." I replied. "We only wish not to be caught, or have our necks stretched. I was about to try my luck with the door, when your sudden arrival stopped me. If the door is not latched, I was going to open it a crack and take a peek, just to be sure, it's the queen's room. Then... I have no idea..."

Jordaar wanted to take command, and opening his beak he shouted, "So do it."

My hand shook slightly as I grasped the latch, and holding my breath, I pushed the lever and pulled the door gently open a crack. I listened for the sound of alarm, but all was quiet. Pressing an eye to the sliver of light that fell from the edge of the door, I peered into a dim lit room. All I could see was a tall backed armchair, facing a very high bed that had steps.

My heart beating faster, I opened the door further. Sticking my head through the opening, I peered right and then left. It appeared no one was in the room. Then a loud snort of snoring erupted into the quietness of the room. Looking at Miiliinda, I pressed a forefinger to my lips, in a sign of silence. I moved the door open enough to squeeze through, and stepped into a fragrant filled room, of sweet smelling incense.

Jordaar flew past my head and settled on the top of one of the four large corner post of the enormous bed. From there he had a birds-eye view of the entire room. He said in his gravelly voice, "It is Queen Gurgold that lies there snoring."

I moved toward the bed using the tall armchair to shield myself. Miiliinda went to the opposite side and matched my movements. Warily, we slowly closed on the bed, ready to flee at a moments notice, or the first outcry. So far, we had been extremely lucky or maybe good fortune had smiled on us.

Reaching the steps at the beds edge, I put one foot on the first step, and the other foot on the next step, until I stood on the topmost step, looking down at an exposed fat leg sticking out from under the bed covering. Her sprawled body lay angled awkwardly, across the bed, arms flung wide.

I leaned forward to look for the necklace and the sour smell of wine assailed my nose. Stifling a cough, I moved closer. Her long black hair covered her face. As I put more of my weight on the mattress, she turned in her stupor and an arm lay across my hand. *Damn.* She was close enough now I could see her throat. I noticed first the fat wrinkled neck that lay bare and... *Her neck was bare.* It was unadorned by the necklace. Perhaps she had taken it off in her drunkenness. I showed my empty hands to the others, and with a shrug of my shoulders whispered, look around for the necklace with the key.

Jordaar swiveled his feathered head cocked an eye and said, "I see something shiny sticking out from beneath her head. Take a look."

Sure enough, it appeared to be a necklace that her head rested upon. I was so close, if she opened her eyes, I would be caught. The smell of her sour breath was strong. I reached for the gold chain... she suddenly gave a loud snore and turned onto her side. The necklace laid exposed ready for the taking. As I picked up the dainty chain, a small key slid from its broken end and fell back onto the bed. *Damn the luck.*

Gurgold started to thrash about. *She must be dreaming.* As I fumbled in the folds of bedding, my hand closed around the tiny key. Slowly I edged from the bed. I pointed my hand to the door and Miiliinda understood. We were out the door in an instant along with Jordaar winging out ahead of us.

I heard a gasp or hopefully only a snore, as I closed the door to the queen's room. I moved quickly but silently to the small window. Miiliinda was already halfway through, and with the help of a push, she sprawled out un-lady like, onto the carpeted hallway.

Miiliinda stood quickly, grasped my wrist and pulled helping me through the open window. I wiggled the last few inches through and fell, my hands touched the floor followed by my feet. I stood taking a deep breath, relieved.

Miiliinda said "Don't just stand there. Let us be gone before someone sounds the alarm." She grabbed my hand and we rushed down the hallway which seemed longer than when we had traversed its length earlier. We had to quickly get out of this hallway, into the stairwell.

We saw no guards before reaching the door that led into the dark stairwell. I whispered to Miiliinda, "Take care of where you step, remember, there is not a handrail on these stairs." Her grip on my hand tightened as she mumbled something in reply. Groping our way along and keeping close to the cold stone of the wall, she led the way down. We arrived at the bottom of the stairwell, found the outer door, opened it cautiously, and peered out into the blackness of the night. I didn't see any guards. We sure didn't want to stumble across a guard patrol at this moment. We edged through the open door into the quiet darkness of night.

A piercing scream cut through the stillness of the night, coming from the queen's balcony above ***"GUARDS, ALL GUARDS ALERT!*** This is the queen. There is an intruder in the castle or on the grounds. Capture them immediately or heads will roll.

We had been discovered. My only thoughts now were to avoid capture and to get as far away from the castle as fast as our legs would carry us. I had no idea where Jordaar had gone. Perched in a tree close by I hoped. I could use his help and his eyes, to make sure we did not run into the palace guards. I reached out with a thought towards him. A quick answer came.

"Yes, I am close. What do you want Alaric?"

"I need your eyes. I want you to fly around and look for the palace guards. If you see any let me know immediately, how many, and how they are placed. I need to know, so that we may avoid them. Can you do that?"

"Yes, if it will help to hasten my transformation back to human form, I'm your man, er, raven. I'm already on the wing, looking." I heard a quick flap of wings; he must have been close by. However, in the dark, I could not see him, for his black feathers blended perfectly into the dark of the night.

With Jordaar's eyes showing us the way, we avoided all the patrols except one. A ten-man patrol was headed straight for us in the wooded area we were working our way out of. When they caught sight of us, they ordered us to surrender or prepare to meet our maker.

Suddenly, from out of the dark came the sound of many flapping wings, along with the screeching caws of ravens. Captain Jordaar, it seems, had recruited all the ravens that had been near. They flew screeching and pecking at the guard's heads blinding and cowered them long enough for us to make good our escape. Soon we were back in the city, safe for the present.

Chapter 13

no Grand Plan

In the early pre-dawn, the sky had lightened to a murky grey, before the sun peeked over the far eastern horizon, streaking it with pale blue. In a quiet voice, Miiliinda and I discussed plans for saving Emerauld. We sat at a small wood table drinking Coffee, in front of a small local cafe that had opened early. Raddick rested with his head on his paws close by our feet on the cold stone sidewalk. The sun rose slowly into the sky, casting its rays across the rooftops. Captain Jordaar sat perched on the limb of a nearby tree his black wing feathers glistening in the early sun.

With my mind, I spoke to the raven, the wolf, and in a low voice to Miiliinda. I didn't wish to be heard by those that might be listing. I asked, "Well, anyone have any ideas, of how we should go about this rescue, without running afoul of Queen Gurgold. All suggestions will be considered, so if you have any let's hear them." I lifted my cup, took a drink, and waited. For a moment, all were silent, obviously thinking. Then everyone spoke at the same time. "Wait... Wait, one at a time please.

Miiliinda said, "Why do we not go there now, is it far?"

"A few days journey at most." I said.

The Captain said, "I have no doubt the queen has already placed a bounty on our heads. She will surly be scouring the city and countryside near and far looking for us. With that quandary, we should probably get to moving on."

"Yes, for sure we should get on with it." I agreed.

Miiliinda interjected. "Well I for one am not going anywhere until the rumbling in my stomach is satisfied." Raddick gave a low growl of agreement; I guess he was hungry too.

We ordered two bowls of porridge with bread that was fresh from an old brick oven. For Raddick a chunk of meat, and since being changed into a wolf, he now liked his meat raw. While we ate, we discussed our strategy. Occasionally I would toss breadcrumbs onto the stone walk. The Captain flew down from his branch and as he strutted about, the crumbs disappeared rapidly.

In the Course of conversation, I remembered Vaadar at the trading post. He seemed not to be happy with the way Queen Gurgold ruled the kingdom. I wondered if he would help. I bet he would help us and I said as much to the others. We needed supplies for two days anyway. With our stomachs full, the four of us set off. Doing our best to avoid the many guardsmen who searched for us, we made our way furtively, through the back streets and alleyways. An hour later, we arrived at Vaadars store. We found Vaadar already up early and open for business. He remembered me.

With surprise showing in his voice, he greeted me with a large smile and hug. "My friend Alaric... what brings you to my humble abode so early in the day? And who is this pretty lady with you? He gave Miiliinda a quick look. Then he noticed the wolf, my brother, standing between Miiliinda and me. His mouth flew open to speak... but closed quickly with a startled expression, as the Captain flew in through the open door and landed with a squawk on the counter. He cocked an eye up at Vaadar and let out another caw. Vaadar was taken by surprise. He paused only for a moment, before stepping forward to shoo the raven away.

"Hold on there Vaadar." I said. "The raven is with me." I spoke to late, for he swung through empty air, as the Captain departed the counter to take refuge on my shoulder. Turning his shiny black head, he stared for a second with his beady eyes and then started scolding Vaadar, cawing loudly, several times.

Vaadar, frowning asked, "What... the devil is all this about?"

"You see, were on a mission to save the rightful queen and the country. We would surely love to have your help."

"Please to explain." Vaadar folded his large arms across his barrel chest and stood waiting.

"You remembered when I bought those supplies from you to go on my excursion exploring the countryside?"

"Yes, yes, I remember like it was yesterday, but that does not explain the girl, the wolf, nor the raven. So yes, I do remember as I said. So do be kind to an old humble goods trader and explain." His bearded face crinkled with a smile. "I do love a good story and this appears to be an extraordinary one, I'd say."

To make Vaadar happy and enlist his aid, I related my entire adventure. When I had finished I said, "When I was here before there was something you said. If I remembered correctly, you said how much you hated Queen Gurgold and what she had done to the country, poverty, high taxes and all. You mentioned too, you would do anything in your power to dethrone her. You remember?"

"That I surly do." He replied with his gruff voice. "What do you have in mind?"

"As we speak Queen Gurgold has her Elite Guards searching for us. What I need are several men to help us set Emerauld free. That's when I thought of you. You know everyone in this part of the country. What say you, will you help us?"

In his booming voice, he said, "For gods' sake man why didn't you say that to start with. I'd do almost anything to get rid of that woman, who calls herself Queen, especially if I can replace her with the rightful heir to the throne. I'm in for a penny or a pound, as the old saying goes. Do you have a plan?"

"We have just stolen a key that will set Emerauld free, but first we must get to her before it's of any use. The Queen has many of her guardsmen looking for us. We will have to be careful not to run afoul of them,"

Stroking his beard, Vaadar deep in thought, grunted, "We will need more help than the five of us. Wait here, I will be right back." He stepped from behind the counter and strode out through the front door.

We heard loud voices coming from the street. A short time passed. Herded by Vaadar, several of the ugly, unkempt ruffians, who usually hung around all-day doing nothing, were pushed through the open door. There must have been seven or eight of them standing in the center of the room.

Vaadars voice boomed, "I found these men just lolling about on the crates in the alleyway. A few were nervous upon seeing you walk into my store. They remembered what happened the last time you were here. I told them why you were here, and all except for a couple, were anxious to volunteer in helping save the rightful Queen." He looked over as a couple more men wandered in. "I see you changed your minds." he said. They didn't answer as they crowded in with the others.

Packing two mules with supplies, our vagabond group started out on foot. We were on our way to save the real Queen, and to right all the wrongs. I instructed the Captain to fly ahead, and report to me if he saw any guards from his lofty place high above the earth. Away he flew on his mission. Raddick loped on ahead to see what he would run across.

An hour later, dodging around large trees which grew thick in this part of the forest we managed to avoid a group of guards, due to the Captains' quick warning. We were now well on our way to leaving the city behind, for the fresh countryside.

I led the group towards the Weettan River, which would take us a few days to reach. I wondered as we strode onward, how we would get across it this time. We were far from the city, so we should not run afoul of the Queens' Guard. Nevertheless, I kept a sharp lookout for them.

Crossing the river would become more of a challenge this time, I was sure. However, I did have some magical powers that might be of use. Then too, there was Miiliinda with her powers. Between the two of us, I was sure we could figure out something.

After three days of trekking, we reached the great river Weettan, just as the sun merged with the horizon streaking the sky with slashes of crimson red. It would soon be dark. There was nothing further we could do this evening. We would have to wait until tomorrow. Unpacking the mules we made camp, lit a fire, cooked food, then our small group sat around the fire eating and talking about how to free Emerauld.

I said, "There are many pitfalls to be aware of. Let me tell you of the ones I know." I told them of the fabulous gemstones. That were cursed and scattered about haphazardly, amongst the giant crystals. The crystals which had trapped and held encase, many different people, including Tagg.

Chapter 14

an Ice River ~ Pursuit

The next morning we faced the prospect of getting across this mighty river where so many had met their demise. Miiliinda and I looked at one another and I asked, "Any ideas?" She looked a little bewildered and said, "Maybe we could conjure up a bridge. Then again, I guess it's probably far too wide to accomplish with my powers." Without thinking, she bent and picked up a stone and in frustration tossed it into the rushing waters. It immediately disappeared with hardly a splash. Her face lit up in a smile and she said, "Maybe I could freeze it. You know turn it into ice."

"It might work. Why not give it a try." I replied.

Vaadar, pulling on his beard with a thoughtful look, stood quietly listening to us. Then he spoke, "She can do this?"

"We will see. Miiliinda, whatever you're going to do, let it rip."

Miiliinda pick up another stone. Clasping it between her two hands, she uttered an incantation, in a language which no one understood. Then she flung the stone far out into the river. Amazingly, the stone didn't sink, but floated on the surface for a second. A golden ripple spread from the stone turning the waters golden. Then the water started spinning, faster and faster forming a whirlpool. Suddenly it turned white freezing. A sheet of ice formed across the surface of the river from bank to bank.

The mighty Weettan River tore and shredded the thin ice into small chunks, which floated downstream. The force of the current was too much for the thin sheet of ice which had covered its surface. The happiness that was on our faces as the river turned to ice was quickly replaced by hopelessness.

Vaadar shrugged his huge shoulders, and in a booming voice said to Miiliinda, "I have never seen such a wonder in all my days. How did you do that?"

"Magic," she answered. "Which wasn't powerful enough it seems. Well I tried."

Vaadar said, "Well, it did work for awhile, but the ice was not thick enough, nor strong enough, to support our weight. You will just have to make it stronger."

Miiliinda turned to me. "Alaric my magic is not powerful enough to overcome the turbulent waters of this mighty river. I will need your help in overcoming it. You said you have some magic powers, which Emerauld gave to you. Do you think we could someway combine our power? With our powers combined we might make the ice strong enough to hold up, long enough for us to cross?"

"I'm not sure how to do that, but we can try," I said. Neither of us was that adept at using our powers of magic, let along trying to combine them. If we did figure out how to combine powers, which was doubtful, who new what might happen? She was more familiar with her power than I was with mine. "So, do you have any ideas?"

"We could hold hands." She said, looking up at me, shyly.

I looked at Miiliinda and said, "This is no time for romance. We must find a way across before Gurgold's guards find us. They surely haven't given up the chase, this soon."

"Of course you're right Alaric; I didn't mean for us to hold hands in a romantic way. I meant so our bodies would be in contact, and connected as one, and then maybe our minds also could be merged into a stronger force. If that works, we would have twice the power as one. Don't you see?"

"Sorry, I wasn't thinking. Shall we dance?" I said in jest, as I reached for her dainty hand. For a moment, I thought she was going to hit me, and then she extended her hand. Her small hand was warm as I held it gently in mine. "Alright I am ready, what do we do now? I don't feel your power. Do you feel anything from me?"

"No, I feel nothing." She replied.

"Well?"

"Stop talking, I'm trying to think." she closed her eyes and thought of her mother, and what her mother had said when she was a little girl. 'Now what was it she had told me when I was a little one.' She said to herself. Suddenly she remembered the phrase, *one person may be weak, but together, many people are strong.*

"Okay, I think this is what we should do. All of us will hold hands in a large circle and give to the person on their left all the power you can project into them. I will stand on one side of the circle and Alaric will stand halfway around on the other side. In that way, we can help the power to flow around and around until I feel it's strong enough."

Everyone gather and form a circle. We all joined hands as ordered, and Miiliinda started the flow with her power. Nothing seemed to happen at first. Then everyone got into it and really started to concentrate. The current began flowing faster and faster as it jumped from person to person. It began building power as it swirled around and around through the circle of people gathering more and more power by the second.

Finally, Miiliinda broke the chain. She bent, picked up a stone which turned a glowing red, blazing with fire. She had sent all the power collected from the group into the stone, which had rested beneath her foot. She held it gentle between her hands as if afraid it would break. Imbuing it with magical words, she tossed it far out into the rushing waters of the river.

The stone left Miiliinda's hand, flying through the air the stone turned an even brighter red, glowing as if afire. It splashed as it hit the rushing waters, and a thin sheet of ice immediately formed across its surface, from bank to bank. Before the river could rip the thin ice apart, the stone sank further changing colors several times, and with each color change, another ice sheet was formed, strengthening the top layer.

After reaching a thickness of fifteen feet, the ice no longer was forming. It appeared to be a miracle, but it was only magic. In awe, everyone gasped in wonder, not ever having seen such an occurrence in their lifetime.

"Everyone hurry; let's get the animals and ourselves across this angry river before the ice melts and breaks up." Helping the mules, stay upright with a lot of pulling and pushing was not an easy task. A few of us didn't fair so well, falling and bruising our buttocks on the slippery ice. Sliding, skidding, and waving our arms trying to keep our balance we reached the other side.

Once everyone was safely across the bridge of ice and standing with solid ground beneath their feet, We looked back toward the river, as the ice screeched, and began to brake apart in large chunks, which immediately, bobbed merry along, on their way downstream.

Everyone gave a shout of victory, along with a rousing cheer that the ordeal was over and everyone had survived.

We rested for a short time after we were across the ice bridge. Then we forged onward towards Zantarre and The Crystal Cave. I wondered what other obstacles we might have to overcome. Raddick had taken off roaming. He was to scout the countryside in search of danger. Nevertheless, for the time being we were free to travel on and we no longer had to worry about being caught by the Queens' Guardsmen.

Off we went in twos and threes, some still talking and others in our motley crew were complaining as we continued on at a moderate pace. A few in our ragtag group continued talking to while away the time, while the others began squabbling about anything, and everything, the sands blowing, how it was to hot to be walking. After a time with the sweat trickling from foreheads, all conversation ceased, as we trudged on.

Then someone started singing, making up the words as they went along. Shortly most of the rest joined in, following the one that had made up the refrain.

Were off—were off

To save the Queen—the Queen

The rightful Queen—you see—you see

A fair—just, and gentle Queen

She will be—will be.

Soon the whole group joined in, singing and swinging their arms. The spirit of the grumbling group had lightened. The pace quicken somewhat, due I'm sure to the mood shift. Our endeavor had somehow taken on a life of its own; it had turned into a fun adventure.

Three hot, dusty days after leaving the river, we came to the base of the mountain called Zantarre. The three of us, Miiliinda, Vaadar and I held a quick meeting. The other men stood about listening while we discussed whether to keep going and start up the mountainside or wait until morning. We decided it best to wait and climb the mountain tomorrow, as the sun was getting preciously close to the horizon, and it would soon be dark.

Several small trees grew at the mountains edge, kept green by a trickle of water that found its way down the mountainside. Beneath the trees were a few clumps of green grass spotted here and there by brown patches of dead grass. I thought it would likely be enough for the mules to feed on. We removed the supplies from the mules and quickly set up camp, as the sky turned darker.

~ ~ ~

Being this close to freeing the true queen everyone was cheerful and in good sprits the next morning. The sunrise was bright and it appeared it was going to be another glorious day, although it would get a lot warmer later on. By which time, I hoped we would be in the coolness of the cave, and well on our way down the tunnel, which led to the large cavern that held our queen, the woman I loved.

We left the mules tied to the trees. There was a small pile of supplies that we left for our return to the city. We had barely started up the mountain when Miiliinda spoke. "Alaric what's that?" she asked, pointing off into the distance. Something had caught her eye. I put a hand up shading my eyes and stared off over the hilly terrain in the direction she pointed. At this distance, I could only make out a dark smudge over the rolling hills. Whatever it was, It was to far off for me to tell what it might be, then it suddenly disappeared below a hill. *Strange.*

I looked sometimes in the direction of the distant hill, where we had first spotted the dark smudge, which had so mysteriously disappeared. We kept moving up the steep slope, getting ever higher and higher. The higher up the rugged mountain we progressed, the farther into the distance I could see.

The smudge kept nagging at my mind. I stopped and looking in the general direction of where we had first sighted the spot I studied it for some time. I wondered what it might be. Then I saw it again. It looked like the smudge was closer, but it was still to far away for me to make out details. As we continued working our way up the steep mountainside, I kept watch on the dark spot. Finally, I could make out that it was a group of riders, still to far away to determine anything of what they were about.

A third of our way up the mountainside to where the cave opening was, I glanced again, to where I had sighted the riders. They were moving rapidly in our direction. I caught a glint of metal reflected from the sun as they grew closer. Then I saw several more bright reflections, coming from at least twelve metal helmets worn by the elite, Queens Mounted Guardsmen. It dawned on me that we were the quarry.

I yelled to the group, "Hells a-foot men, the Queens' Guard has found us. Let us not dally any longer." *I thought, if they caught us we would be arrested and probably hung, if I knew Gurgold.* "Hurry along men. The cave is not much further. We must get to Emerauld before they catch us." The thought of getting captured, was unbearable, when I was this close to saving Emerauld. It drove me to push everyone even harder, to their limits.

We were almost to the cave when I looked back, down the mountain towards our pursuers. The guardsmen had reached our campsite, dismounted in one big hurry, and quickly started up the mountain after us. We struggled upward with renewed vigor. They had a ways to go before they would catch us, if they could. We were almost to the cave.

My heart rose in triumph when we reached the cave. The Elite Guards were not close enough to stop us now. Then I looked at the opening, which had completely filled with dirt and rocks, my heart fell. I thought something like this might occur, and had prepared, bringing shovels.

I called to Vaadar, "Have Jeenfaller and a couple of his men clear the way under those two boulders." I said. "Tell them to hurry, and to dig fast if they don't want to be hung."

Vaadar quickly set the men to digging. I kept an eye on the approaching guardsmen as they drew ever nearer; it had become a deadly race. "Hurry it up men!" I desperately shouted, "They are almost upon us."

It was going to be close. "Dig faster, men," I urged the diggers. They heeded my advice. The diggers picked up the pace. Shoveling furiously, dirt flew in every direction. It was a race, to see if we could save our necks from stretching.

The opening between the clasped hands, of the two boulders, protecting the entrance grew larger by the second. When the opening was large enough, we sent Miiliinda through first. Then one man at a time quickly followed. They squeezed through the tight opening shoving the shovels ahead and disregarding the dirt. They in turn helped the next one up through the opening. I took a quick glance at the guards who were almost upon us. Then movement further out on the plain caught my eye. A great number of foot soldiers marched towards us.

With a lump in my throat, I dove for the hole and scrambled through last. I had barely made it under the clasped boulders in time. That was close. I felt elated being last through and avoiding capture, then a hand suddenly grabbed on to my boot. I yelled and kicked hard at the hand with my other boot. I was rewarded with a muffled yell of pain, coming from without. I smiled.

Chapter 15

~ the key to Freedom ~

The tunnel was dark. Someone lit a lantern. I stared into the dirty, sweat stained faces of the group. They all stared back. Relieved, they stood awaiting my instructions, and all had a smile on their face, even Vaadar.

Vaadar coughing asked, "What now my friend? We have eluded the guard for the time. But now we are trapped in this dark, dank... he coughed... tunnel."

"Ah, Vaadar, where is your faith? You trust me, yes."

"Yes, Alaric, but there is something you should know."

"Alright tell me. What is it I should know?"

"There is someone coming through the opening."

I looked down to the opening where we had crawled up from and saw a hand, then an arm. I grabbed a shovel from a man and seeing Jeenfaller still holding his shovel, I yelled. "Jeenfaller, we must fill the opening quickly." I started shoveling dirt on the hand and Jeenfaller joined me. Being a large man, he shoveled twice the dirt. The arm we had seen was removed rapidly. Another man joined us and the three of us rapidly filled in the hole, tossing in several large rocks as we shoveled. After a few minutes I said, "That should slow them down and hold them for a time."

Vaadar stood holding a lantern and watched as we filled in the opening. When we were done, without a word he stepped onto the mound of dirt and with his substantial weight stomped it tight, making it harder for the guards to dig through. When he was satisfied he grunted and said, "That should hold them for awhile. I doubt they have shovels so they will have to use knives and their hands. He looked at me and lighting a second lantern handed it to me. "Lead on, Alaric, I will protect the rear."

"You're a good man." I said. Taking the lantern, I led the way down the tunnel, the soft glow it cast, illuminating our way. Some time later, we arrived to where the tunnel split into two different directions. Remembering, the branch to the right was the one I had taken, I led the group down it through the many twist and turns it made.

I knew the Elite Guard would not stop untill we were captured, but so far there was no sign of pursuit. After traversing several bends, I saw a faint glow of light coming from far ahead, reflecting around the next bend. Then the voice of Vaadar came echoing to my ear.

"Alaric, I hear the sound of many voices, soon I think, we have unwanted company. Surely we must be close to the cavern."

"How near are the guards?" I said, and then added. "We are almost there. I can see the light coming from the next bend."

"I think guards to far away, but still to close for comfort. Without a lantern to show the way, they struggle along in the dark. I think we reach the light, before they reach us."

We turned the bend, and just steps away, the huge circular boulder sat, blocking the opening of the crystal cave. Grabbing Vaadar by the arm, I dragged him to one side of the boulder. Vaadar there is a lever in this hole. I want you to reach in and pull it when I give the signal, okay.

"Vaadar nodded and quickly reach into the hole and waited for my signal. I rushed to the opposite side. Making haste, I felt around until I found the right opening. Reached in grabbed the lever, and pulling hard, I yelled. "Pull, Vaadar, pull." The boulder made a grinding sound and started to roll back into the caves wall. Soon the entrance lay exposed and open.

The light, cast from the many glittering crystals, was blinding as it poured forth through the opening. Directly in front of me I saw Tagg, his eyes wide in joy. still holding the red stone high, still encased in the crystal.

Then I remembered. "Stop," I yelled, spreading my arms wide. As I gazed at Tagg tears came to my eyes. He was just as I had left him, how many days ago. I did not want to see anyone receive the same fate as Tagg.

I warned everyone not to enter, and if they did to stay directly behind me. One failed to obey, and greedy rushed forward, grabbed a large yellow stone from the ground, and was immediately turned into a large yellow tinged crystal.

Everyone had slowly been edging forward, mouths agape at all the jewels that lay about ripe for the picking. Upon seeing their friend encased and turned into a giant crystal, they froze in fear. I quieted their fears telling them no harm would come to them if they obeyed and followed my orders. I ordered the men that held shovels, to move the boulder and close off the opening, if they could.

Then the crystals started changing, slowly taking on a green tinge, as I spoke. The men stood watching in awe and amazement, as a large golden throne arose, from amidst the jumbled crystals.

Emerauld, seated upon the throne stood as the throne stopped rising. She surveyed the group and then her gaze fell on me. "Ah, Alaric." a voice in my head said, "I see you have returned and brought others. I sense that one among you has the power to do magic."

"Yes, that is true my Queen. Let me introduce to you, Miiliinda. Without her help, we would not be here now to greet our *True* Queen."

Miiliinda stepped forward and bowed her head graciously. Emerauld smiled, then nodded in return, and asked. "Alaric did you accomplish your mission? Did you bring the key, which will lift this cursed spell that binds and holds me?" She asked anxiously. "The key will set me free to pursue my path to real freedom?"

I held up my hand. Dangling from my fingertips was a gold chain with a tiny gold key attached.

Her smile broadened into a wide grin which suddenly changed to a frown. "I sense there are others coming. You must hurry, for they are almost upon us. Come to me and unlock this necklace from around my throat.

Afraid to move, the others could only watched as she guided me step by step keeping me safe, until at last I stood beside her. The men found their voices and cheered. The cheering went unnoticed. Emerauld looked into my eyes, and I looked into hers for a moment. Then I reached for her necklace and inserted the key into the tiny lock. Hearing the sound of many voices, I paused. There followed loud cursing, followed by angry shouts. Then everything erupted into complete chaos. The guards had somehow found a way past the boulder. Shouting in triumph, they came surging in creating havoc among the men. Vaadar and his men fought valiantly, desperate to secure the entrance, giving me more time.

Emerauld brought me back to reality, I quickly turned the key. The lock sprung open and fell to the floor, along with the necklace. Emerauld was free for the time being, of the spell, which had kept her prisoner for all these years.

She pointed at the guards who had entered and were trying to kill Vaadar and his men. She uttered several words which I did not understand. The guards and Vaadars men were all frozen in mid-action. Some with swords raised high, others frozen in mid swing with closed fist.

She looked at me and smiled. "There, now we have time." Putting her arms around my neck, she pulled me close. "I will not forget what you have done for me and the kingdom." Our lips touched. A flash of brilliant white light swirled around in my head, followed quickly after by an unusual tingle. Whatever it was it didn't last long.

Her gaze wandered around the cavern, which had been her prison for such a long time. Finally her eyes stopped, coming to rest on the giant crystals. Looking at the crystals, she raised both arms towards them and angrily uttered several short words. To my surprise, I could now understand. She had given me more than just a kiss that had left me tingling. She had imbued me with more power and knowledge of the magic.

With a flick of her hand, all of the many colored jewels, that lay scattered about, started to rise from the floor. As the stones started upward, she flicked her other hand in a circle. The colored stones glittered even more, as they started to spin individually, in ever-widening circles as they rose higher and higher. Brilliant flashes of light bounced from the ceiling and walls of the cavern. Indeed, it was a magnificence sight to behold.

As the stones spun ever higher and higher, they soon became more and more erratic. They began crashing into the giant crystals shattering them like glass. The noise was almost unbearable as the pieces fell to the ground in jumbled heaps, which quickly dissolved and disappeared. It all happened so fast. My mouth opened in awe. I could only stand and watch. I wanted to weep, on seeing the destruction of such great wealth.

The dust from the destruction started to clear somewhat. I was startled to see the many men that had been trapped, still alive waving their arms, trying to clear the dust. Coughing and rubbing their eyes, they looked about, completely disorientated and bewildered. Then my eyes were drawn to one small boy that stood among the rubble, apparently lost. Tagg! My heart leaped, I was overjoyed at seeing him alive. Tagg was not dead. I started for him.

Emerauld grabbed my arm. "Wait."

"But, he's my friend. I'm...

"Just wait. There is no need to hurry, not now that I am free." The dust disappeared immediately with a waved of her arm. She took my hand and led me down from the throne, which was the only thing left standing in the vast cavern, now that the crystals had been destroyed.

The newly freed men warily watched as we approached. They had gathered, conversing and united into a tight group, ready to fight.

Emerauld spoke. "Pease do not be frightened. I will do you no harm. Look around. What do you see? Only yourselves, the citizens of Borrgess, which have been held here in this cavern for far too long. Then there are also some of Queen Gurgold's Elite Guards. Which are no longer hers, they are now mine."

She pivoted toward the guards that stood as statues, frozen in time, waved a hand. Releasing the spell, the guards continued with the fighting. She commanded, "Stop the fighting at once. We are all one." The fighting quickly came to a halt. All eyes turned toward Emerauld. With dignity befitting a queen, she radiated awesome power as she spoke. The intensity of words along with the fire in her eyes, held everyone spellbound. No one moved.

"These are your people, that you would slay, mime or imprison, and for what? For your Queen, my sister Gurgold, who has taken control of your minds and has taken the throne by force. The crown and throne by all rights of law are always bequeathed to the first-born. It is known throughout the kingdom that I am the eldest. Therefore, I claim my rightful heritage to be Queen."

The guards looked at the people, then at each other, as if awakening from a dream. They sheepishly laid down their arms. Her words brought relief and a newfound hope to them all.

"Guards kneel," she commanded.... "Pledge your loyalty to me, Queen Emerauld." All the guards knelt as one. All the others in the cavern knelt also, to honor and pledge their fealty to the rightful queen. Every face glowed with hope.

Chapter 16

~ out from the Dark ~

Something nudged my mind with thoughts. It was the Captain. In all the confusion and excitement I had forgot about him. The raven sat on a branch of the tree where our group had last maid camp. Nearby, the mules were chomping on what little grass there was.

"What is it Captain Jordaar?" My mind responded.

He replied, "The queens army approaches, and are only several meters away. You are going to be trapped in the cave with no way out." There was a pause . . . "You did tell me it was the only entrance and exit, didn't you?"

"We have rescued the *true queen* and overcome all the obstacles that stood in our way. She is saved from the wrath of her sister. Now we shall see what she can and will do. She has magical powers that few have ever seen, so do not worry as to our fate, and Captain do try to stay alive.

"Alaric, I will be your eyes and ears. Fear not, for the soldiers will take no notice of me sitting here quietly in this tree. Oh! One other thing, the clouds are gathering and the sun has hidden. It might get wet, it looks like.

I laughed at the thought of the captain sitting there quietly on a branch, and worrying about getting a little wet. "That would be something to see, you being quiet. You will probable caw at them." Then I laughed again. He must have known I laughed at him. He squawked right back at me, his blasphemous words ringing, as they bounced around in my head.

"The soldiers are here; they're dispersing and starting up the mountainside. Be careful."

I looked at Emerauld; she tilted her head toward me, nodded, smiled and said, "Are you ready to take on the kingdom to reclaim the throne?"

"Lead the way my queen. I am your humble and obedient servant and I await only your orders." My face lit up. A mischievous twinkle came into my eye. Grinning, I bowed with a graceful sweep of an arm, "Your every wish and desire, is only a command away."

Taking her by the arm, I led her through the group of soldiers, Vaadar's thugs, and the newly freed men. All were now united as one. Tagg rushed to greet me. Laughing, he hugged me. I pulled him close to my side smiling at his enthusiasm, and ruffling his hair. Then I hugged him back. "I can't tell you how glad I am to see you're still alive. With Emerauld at my side and Tagg on the other, we walked out of the cavern into the long tunnel on our way to freedom, I hoped."

A soft green glow, emanated from Emerauld, lighting the tunnel and showing the way. Vaadars ruffian group along with the elite guards brought up the rear.

A message erupted in my head. "The soldiers are grouped around the two tall boulders that sit at the entrance to the cave. They have drawn swords. Be very careful you don't lose your head when you come out."

There was a pause... followed by a squawk.

"Captain, what is it?"

Another squawk... "My beautiful shiny feathers are getting wet. The dark clouds are opening and releasing rain. I shall have to find shelter... squawk."

Upon reaching the entrance to the tunnel a short time later, we stopped. "Your sister's army waits for us to come out. Were trapped Emerauld, like rats down a hole. What do we do now? We can't leave here without being captured and maybe losing our heads. There must be hundreds of solders."

"Do you have so little faith in my powers?" She looked at me, smiled and faced toward the two huge boulders, which leaned together sealing the entrance. She reached out her arms towards the boulders, placed her hands together. Speaking in the strange language said. "You have leaned together for long enough, part from one another... Now." She spread her arms and hands wide as she spoke. "Watch."

The ground rumbled and started to shake beneath our feet. The massive boulders started to tremble, as if awaking from a deep sleep. Then slowly they parted and fell, uprooting great chunks of damp earth, taking it with them. Where the boulders had stood was now a large gaping opening, leading to the outside.

The soldiers surrounding the entrance froze as they felt the earth shake. In a panic, their eyes were drawn toward the boulders which had begun to shake. With a great grinding rumble, they toppled, hitting the sloping terrain, bounced once, and started rolling haphazardly, down the wet mountainside.

Regaining their senses, the soldiers quickly jumped back away from the boulders. In a stupor they watched, as the boulders tumbled and rolled, gaining more momentum with each turn. They bounced thundering downhill, taking out many of the soldiers. Others desperately ran for their lives, scattering like ants, whose nest had been disturbed.

The army running in fear was a sight to behold. For the few who weren't fast enough, the boulders rolled over crushing them. Others were lucky, having only been squashed into the muddy earth, soften by the drenching rain. Dripping and covered with mud, those who had survived arose from the mire.

Vaadar bellowed with laughter at the sight. Then our group gave a loud cheer. It was a funny sight to see. The army covered in mud had been disarmed. The muddy soldiers who survived didn't mind the mud, as they knelt, and pledged their loyalty to Queen Emerauld.

The storm clouds drifted off south, driven by a slight breeze. The sun peeked through the thinning clouds, and the sky began to clear.

The Elite Guards moved quickly hurrying to keep up with Emerauld, whose long legs and mind raced swiftly. She thought ahead to the confrontation with her sister. The thought burned in her brain. Following after came Vaadar and his gang of cutthroat, ragtag ruffians. Behind and last, came what was left of the army. Still, a formidable group of muddy, but determined fighting men,.

With long strides, Emerauld, her face set with determination, led the way. We soon arrived at the great river Weettan. The fast moving water roaring as it sped rapidly along. Those who approached to close to the river received a thorough drenching. The river an awesome sight, looked to be as wild as ever, as it rushed past.

Finding a shallow eddy of current behind a jutting bank, some of the soldiers standing knee deep in cold water, washed the mud from themselves and their equipment. Soon others joined in. After the late comers finished rinsing off the clinging mud, a clean presentable army appeared, although wet.

I stood contemplating a moment, thinking about my last crossing and wondered what Emerauld would do. I didn't have long to wait. She laughed at the questioning expression on my face. Then tapping me on the nose with a finger, she smiled and said, "Watch." Turning two times in a circle she stopped and faced the river. Then she did something with her hands and extending her arms forward she uttered an incantation. A large bridge suddenly appeared, spanning the river from bank to bank.

I looked in bewilderment. The bridge was not all that beautiful, it was made of ruff wood planks that arched above the rushing waters, but still, I thought it beautiful. Marching across the bridge, we continued onward across vast fields of wheat, toward the castle.

Coming soon to the outlying farmlands, the good people and peasants both, gathered around to see such a sight. Word spread rapidly ahead that we were taking back the Kingdom. We were on the way to dethrone Queen Gurgold, Emerauld's sister. As we marched across the fields, and through the towns, more and more farmers, villagers, and townspeople joined the march. Our army swelled by the hundreds. No one would dare try to stop us now.

Chapter 17

~ confrontation ~

It started as a low hum, and gradually grew louder and louder, until the words echoed as they were repeated across the countryside. Most all of the common citizens had joined in the chant, "Hang the queen, hang queen Gurold, hang queen Gurold."

Every town we past through, we gathered more citizens into our mass. By the time, we reached the castle, almost everyone that could walk were with us. Surly, none could stand against us. As we approached the gates, they were flung open and we entered into the courtyard, unopposed.

Queen Gurold was not there to greet us or welcome her sister Emerauld, either. In fact, she was not to be found anywhere, as we searched high and low.

King Varnater, her husband, was found hiding in the stables. A saddle lay on the ground between him and a horse that had a twisted bridle around its head. I guess Varnater had no idea of how to saddle and bridle a horse.

Trying to keep her anger in control, Emerauld asked him, "Where has that witch Gurgold gone, the one who I call sister?" She finished the question with a toss of her golden locks. She stood facing a cowering man, who called himself King. She awaited his answer, hands on her hips, a flush of hot anger rising in her face.

Varnater, choked out the words, "She left in the carriage." He hung his head. "Without me... how could she..." He looked up, his eyes glassy, filled with tears, "I have been loyal. I have done everything she commanded of me. Then she just leaves me behind... like an old piece of discarded garbage."

He looked at Emerauld, Wringing his hands, his face twisted in fear, he asked. "What are you going to do with me?" Then he pleaded. "Please, please... do not hang me." As he spoke, the tears ran down his face into his grey streaked beard, a defeated, pathetic looking man.

Anger edging her voice, she asked. "Did you perchance see which road her carriage took?"

He answered haltingly stumbling over his words. "The, the, last, last, I saw of the carriage, it was headed out from the castle, on the little used west road." He was quite a moment and then added, "Where she was going I don't know, but she was in one hell of a great rush." He thought some more. "There's nothing out that direction, except some small hills, which lie just beyond the river Grazalor."

Emerauld turned, a question on her lips, "Alaric, the Captain of the Elite Guard that was appointed by Gurgold, do you trust him?" As the words fell from her lips, and before I could give my answer, Jordaar the raven landed at her feet.

Upon hearing her words, he hopped and strutted about, cawed once and said, "Do you not remember my Queen? I was the former Captain of the Elite Guard. Appointed by your father, King Vaarzen, and I know these guardsmen quite well. They will follow my ever order, just as I obey you and follow your orders, as your loyal and trustworthy servant, so will they obey mine." He tried to bow, but could not, due to being a raven. "Restore me my queen; to human form, I implore you. If anyone can catch her it would surly be me, for all the suffering she has cause us."

"Further more... while winging high up across the vast sky looking for opposition to our forces; I spied the royal carriage, stirring up dust on the old road, headed west." He hopped about, cocked his head and looked up with a beady black eye.

"My queen, I know a short cut behind the castle. I could ride out, through the vales with the Élite Guards. With a little luck we could intercept the carriage and Gurold, and return her forthwith, for your convenience to deal with as you wish."

"What say you... My queen?" He squawked boldly.

Emerauld did not take long to make a decision. She looked down at the large black raven, who didn't know when to stop chattering, as he hopped from one foot to another, awaiting her answer.

With a flourish of her hand, she uttered several mystical words, and immediately, Capitan Jordaar appeared in the middle of a poof of white smoke. Dressed in his full black uniform, shiny buttons and all, like he'd come fresh from the drill field. "Ah, it is good to be back to normal." He said to himself. Now that he was back in the flesh, his demeanor changed. Not quit as cocky as he'd been as a Raven.

He stood smartly at attention, clicked his boot heels, made an elaborate deep bow, straightened and saluted the Queen. He said, "I await only your command, my Queen."

Emerauld faced toward the Elite Guard, saying as she turned, "Guards, put this, this despicable imposter that claims to be your Captain, under arrest. She indicated the traitor which Gurgold had put in charge of the Guardsman. I will deal with his betrayal later. As for you, my dear Captain Jordaar," she paused looking Jordaar straight in the face with her sharp green eyes, until she caught his full attention. "Make hast and retrieve my sister Gurgold and bring her to me. I shall be at the castle, awaiting your swift return Captain. Go! You're dismissed."

With that, she turned after the guards, her long legs carrying her swiftly after them. As she caught up, she noticed the usurper Captain, had been denied the use of his hands, which were bound with rope.

The group continued on, followed by every rank and station of citizen, that had nothing better to do. They trailed along in groups, after the guards, talking amongst themselves. Here and there, a citizen would yell out, "Hang her, hang the witch Gurold." The people were in high sprits hoping to catch queen Gurold. Surely, she would be hung when caught.

At this very moment, Queen Gurgold, in her splendid royal coach of gold and purple, raced for help. To the place in that dark cave where she'd gotten the evil black power, along with her taste for cruelty. Glancing back, she looked for pursuers that might have followed. She didn't want to be caught. Fearing the anger of the citizens, and what might befall her, if they got their hands on her. She shuddered at the thought. She didn't know why but her power to cast spells seemed to be diminishing in strength. She must renew it.

Reaching the castle, Alaric along with the guards escorted King Varnater to a cell, in the lower reaches of the castle. Locking the door, he stopped and said, "Queen Emerauld will decide what to do with you later, and stop your sniveling and act like a man."

He stood a moment looking at the broken man." Who knows? Maybe she will set you free, out of the kindness of her heart. You know, deep down, she is a very caring woman. She is not at all like you or her sister."

He turned and went up the steps in search of the woman he loved. Now that she was a Queen. He wondered where that left him. He supposed he would find out in due time. Right now, they had to catch Gurgold, before she could do more harm.

He found Emerauld at the stables, and was barely in time to watch as Captain Jordaar, trailing a cloud of dust, led the Elite Guardsmen over a hillock. He hoped they would be successful. They moved swiftly out of sight on their way to intercept Gurgold.

Captain Jordaar rode beside each of the guardsmen explaining the shortcut they were taking. How by all means they must get ahead of Gurgold and keep her from escaping. To maybe return at a later time, and turn them all into stone.

Soon they were riding across open meadows, somewhat parallel, but still some distance away from the road that ran close to the river. From the exertion of steady running the horse's coats were beginning to lather showing flecks of white, The horses needed rest, but the Captain would not, could not be stopped. "Hurry men, faster, it's a matter of life or our death." Spurred on by the Captains grim words, they rode over a rise that lay ahead. If the very devil himself were chasing them, they could not have ridden faster.

With the speed their mounts made, luck smiled on them. Off some distance on their right side, and somewhat below where they rode, traveled the royal carriage. Unnoticed, they raced ahead to a small grove of trees where they set up an ambush. They had not long to wait. The carriage came around a large boulder and headed straight for the river.

The Elite Guardsmen quickly surrounded Gurgold's carriage, effectively stopping her from trying to escape across the river, Grazalor. The river was swollen from the recent rains to the north, making it impossible to cross. A Guardsman grabbed the divers whip, and jerked the man from his high perch. He scrambled to his feet dazed from his tumble to the ground. Before he could regain his senses, he was bound hand and foot, unable to defend Gurold.

The carriage door was yanked open by one of the Guardsmen that had surrounded it., Before she could react, two other Guardsmen pulled Gurold from inside. Quickly she was gagged, blindfolded, and bound. It all happened so fast, she had not the time, to cast a spell.

The journey back to the castle was somewhat more leisurely than the chase. Once back inside the castle-keep, the triumphant returning guardsmen were greeted heartily by their fellow guardsmen.

Captain Jordaar dismounted and strode up to Emerauld and saluted. "We have returned with your sister, as you commanded my Queen." As he finished speaking, but before he was dismissed something odd occurred. Emerauld's spell must have worn off, for the Captain had reverted back to the cocky black raven he had once been. He cawed out in anguish.

Emerauld said, "I am sorry Captain, I must have used a temporary spell by mistake. Please forgive me. I shall try my best to make it permanent. For now, I must deal with my sister, the evil one. I am sure you understand."

The poor Captain could only squawk in disappointment.

The ragtag group which had rescued Queen Emerauld stood aside watching as Gurold with her hands still bound, blindfolded and gagged was helped from the carriage. Held by two burly guards she was escorted, and made to stand in front of Queen Emerauld.

"Well my sister, it is so good to see you again, after all this time. Let me see, how long has it been? No need to answer, I remember it all too well."

As Emerauld talked, she strode around her sister, looking her up and down. "All those wasted years, I waited. Oh, how I have waited, for this moment for so long, when we could finally say hello, and see one another again. However, I'm sure, you remember how long."

"What's that you say?" She paused, then in mock horror said, "Oh, my poor sister! What ever have they done to you? Why have they bound and gagged, and blindfolded you? Is it something you have done?"

"Oh, how rude of me, my sweet sister, to ply you with all these questions, when you can only grunt your reply. Here, let me take that filthy rag from your mouth and that horrid blindfold from your eyes."

Several guards and Alaric quickly stepped forward to stop Emerauld, but they were to late. Before anyone could stop her, she reached up with both hands and removed Gurgold's gag and blindfold. The crowd gasped and held their breath, dreading the consequences of her actions.

Gurgold blinded by the bright sun, blinked several times, then opened her mouth to speak. "You"... was the only word to leave her lips, when Emerauld's hand swiftly and effectively clamped tight across the mouth, shutting off any further words.

The guards held tight as Gurgold struggled to break free. The green eyes of Emerauld glittered as they bore into those of her sister with an intense hypnotic gaze. She leaned close to her struggling sister, and whispered an incantation into her ear. With the casting of the spell her sister was deprived of all the evil powers, she had controlled, or maybe, the evil powers had controlled her.

Emerauld removed her hand and stepped back. "Release her." She commanded the guards. The two guards hesitated, and looked at one another, in doubt. Emerauld smiled, and gave a nod. The guards removed the ropes that restrained Gurgold's hands. Several, but not everyone in the watching crowd, took a step back as the ropes hit the ground.

Gurgold was free. She stood there for a moment, then raised a hand and opened her mouth to cast a spell. She only uttered gibberish, which not even the evil powered one would understand. She raise her other hand and with both hands, she tried again to cast a spell. Everyone held their breath in fear. Nothing happened. Gurgold's power was gone.

The crowd hesitantly followed timidly behind the brave Elite Guards, who had captured and subdued Gurgold. As they led her toward the castle, a great sigh of relief arose from the huge crowd of citizens and farmers. Then a voiced shouted out, "Hang her. Hang the witch, before she causes anymore trouble." Soon others in the crowd picked up the chant and joined in, shouting "Hang her, Hang her now."

The brave souls who had rescued one Queen, and subdued another, were lost from sight of the crowd, as the massive steel banded oak doors of the castle, closed slowly, behind them.

Chapter 18

~ decisions ~

Gurgold was escorted to the room she had occupied as a child. The door was locked and the key pocketed by Emerauld. To make sure she had no chance of escaping, two guards were then stationed at the door

"Let us retire to the meeting room by the great hall, so we may discuss the situation. Shall we?" No one moved. "Well?"

Still no one moved then Alaric spoke up. "Emerauld, my Queen, if you would be kind enough to lead the way, we will follow. For I am almost certain, none of us have ever been in such a grand castle as this." Everyone in the group nodded in assent except for one. Tagg was staring open mouth. in wonder, at all the pictures hung on the walls. Most were portraits of kings and queens of long past era's.

The entourage moved to follow the queen and I called to Tagg, "Tagg, don't dally, hurry along. We must keep up with the queen, or we surely will become lost, in this maze of stone and mortar, and might never find our way out."

Tagg and I trailed after the group, into a room maybe thirty by fifty feet. Tagg looked around. More paintings hung on the walls. I thought if this is but a small meeting room, what size, must the great hall be. *I wondered.*

Emerauld seated herself at the head of a large oval table that was so highly polished you could see your face reflected in its shining surface. The table could easily hold forty people or more. Emerauld said, "Everyone please sit. She caught my eye and indicated the chair to her right. Alaric, sit here beside me, and Tagg, you may take the seat here on my left."

The others with their dirt-smeared faces didn't look much better than Miiliinda. Soon all had found a chair in which to sit. Then they tried their best to get comfortable in the tall straight back chairs. The white wolf lay on the stone floor close behind Miiliinda's chair, and the raven perched himself on an empty chair back

All heads turned toward Emerauld, as she spoke. "My brave friends... for rescuing me, I give you all... my deepest thanks. And, especially to you Alaric, for discovering my plight, and then putting our plan into action, and bringing that plan to fruition. And we all should be thankful we are still alive." She smiled. All the dirty faces smiled back in agreement.

"Now then, we, or should I say, I have only begun the task that lies before me." She looked at the faces which now had great concern reflected on them. "I, with your help, will set the Kingdom, and the people, on the right path to peace and prosperity. What do you say? Are you with me?" Everyone gave their voice of approval in a loud shout of yeas, except for two. One gave a loud caw and the other gave a deep-throated growl.

Although, Emerauld had yet to be crowned by a lawful coronation, she acted with grace and compassion, as befitted a Queen, *the rightful Queen*. She said, "First, I have been remiss, concerning our two brothers, who without their help, we could not have come this far."

Scratching his beard, Vaadar look puzzled. The others looked at each other wondering. Emerauld, laughed at their confused looks. Then she said, "Have you forgotten our friends that carry a worst burden and curse than all of us. I speak of the white wolf and the black raven, Alaric's brother Raddick, and Captain Jordaar, both of whom are trapped in bodies not of their own choosing."

The Queen shoved back her chair and went to the wolf, knelt, and stroking Raddick's head. She uttered several words in the strange language, as she ran a hand down his back. Then she stood, snapped her fingers, folded her arms and waited. All had turned in their chairs to watch. Nothing changed for an instant, and then suddenly the wolf became obscured in a cloud of glittering swirling white. Then clearing, it revealed a strikingly, handsome young man. Raddick stood where the wolf had been.

At this wondrous display of magic, the watchers rose from their chairs awed, then they applauded, shouting hurray.

Raddick bowed low before Emerauld in humble gratitude. She reached out her hand to Raddick as he came to attention with a click of his boots; He very gently grasped the offered hand, and with some trepidation bowed and kissed it. He said, "Thank you, your majesty." She waved him off.

Dismissed, he turned and went immediately to Miiliinda, and taking her dainty hand in his, he kissed it. "Although you are not a Queen, I have wanted to do that, since I first laid eyes on you."

She looked down, blushing at his boldness. She raised her head, pushed her long dark locks from her face and glazed into his handsome and gentle smiling face. Two bright brown eyes stared back, tinged with humor, they watched closely for her reaction.

She smiled at Raddick and her eyes grew misty, brimming over with tears of happiness. He still held her hand which trembled ever so slightly, and she said haltingly, "Raddick, I..." she stumbled over her words, "You are, so... so... well, more than I expected."

The queen turned away from them. She pointed her finger at Jordaar, who was still perched on the chair back. "And you, Captain of the Elite Guards," Her finger shook, as if she were reprimanding a small child, and her green eyes brightened mischievously. She spoke in the strange language and with a slight movement of her hand, she threw a bolt of blinding white light, it flew straight hitting the raven.

Blinded only for an instant none could believe what they saw. The light had knocked the raven from his perch on the chair. Stunned, he toppled backwards from the chair falling. Before he hit the floor, he was transformed back to his normal self.

Standing he proceeded to brush himself off. Before he could address the Queen, someone started to laugh. The Captain, who was always so prim and proper, his uniform dusty and in disarray, presented a comical sight. Soon all were laughing.

The Captain grimaced not looking at those that laughed. Then he bowed to Emerauld, straightened, gave a quick salute and said, "My Queen, words cannot express the thanks and the gratude I feel, being myself again, for the second time. I am at your command."

"First, you should gather around you the guardsmen who are loyal to you, the ones you can truly trust. And the ones you don't trust... or are not sure of... lock them away in the dungeon. Their fate will be decided later." While you are down there, see if there are any who Gurgold has put there without a just cause. Use your discretion to free those that have been done an injustice. Go now!"

Captain Jordaar turned on his heel and strode from the room on his way to implement the Queens orders.

"Now then where was I? Oh, yes, what of my sister's fate. I cannot just hang her as the citizens want. There surely must be an alternate way... to punish her for her misdeeds, and the hardship she has caused the people." She wiped a tear from the corner of her eye, then stammered, "I... I... You see, I still love my sister in spite of everything she has done.

I feel I must ask for your advice, and counsel, as you are now my new friends. I seek another solution to that of hanging her. What say you my friends?" Silence filled the room as everyone looked thoughtful. Then one after the other turned to his neighbor to discuss the best way to avoid the hanging, the citizens had decreed. Soon the sound of many voices filled the room. Emerauld sat looking hopefully from one person to the next.

Emerauld stood finally and waved her hands for silence. "Well, if anyone has an idea or a solution to my problem I would like to hear it, now." The room grew quiet again.

Alaric said, "I have an Idea. Why don't you cast a spell on her as she did on you? Then you could take her to the same cave, where she kept you prisoner for years, I think that would be a befitting punishment." Several men liked what Alaric had suggested and agreed with him wholeheartedly. A yea, was forthcoming from most everyone.

Thinking for a minute Emerauld stood smiling and said, "I like your idea Alaric." So Gurgold's fate was settled, or so everyone thought. About that time, there was a loud commotion coming from the hallway. The door burst open, and Captain Jordaar entered the room. Followed by many men and women, who were dressed in what at one time, must have been royal refinement, but now hung in tatters.

"My Queen, may I present to you some of the dukes,' duchess, princes and princesses from that last unforgettable royal banquet. I am sure you remember only to well, those events, as do I. These are the unfortunate ones, which did not leave the castle quick enough to escape the wrath of Gurgold.

They were imprisoned and locked in the dungeons below. I have set them free at your orders." Emerauld stood dumbfounded, at a loss for words for the moment. She shook her head in anger, for she recognized some, who were friends.

She looked to where several servants stood silent against the walls like statues not moving. Pointing a finger toward them she said, "You, you, and you, kindly assist these nobles. Show them where they may clean themselves. Then find them proper attire, befitting and appropriate for a person of royalty."

The servants moved away from the wall slowly, unsure. Emerauld clapped her hands. "Quickly now," she ordered. "See that you step lively, help our friends so they may be presented properly." The servants jumped quickly, to the task at hand, showing the haggard and grubby royals out of the room. Thinking of the royalty that had been saved from her sister, her spirits lifted somewhat.

Her mood brightened even more, as she looked on the group sitting around the table, the people who had saved her. Then a thought occurred. All eyes were fixed on her. She could see she had their full attention. "Since saving me, and what we have all gone through together, we have become friends. And after our most recent achievement, the finding and freeing of the royals. I think this is a great moment, and most certainly, calls for a celebration, wouldn't you agree?" A roar of cheers, followed by several yeas, agreed with the idea. They deserved it.

$$\sim \sim \sim$$

So, they started on the planning. Emerauld was surprised that there was so much to do in the planning of such a large festival and banquet.

In order to accommodate the citizens of the towns, and the farmers in the outlying countryside, it would have to be held on the grassy slopes of the meadows, which surrounded the castle,

Couriers would have to be sent, to all of the surrounding nobles who had survived Gurgold's rule. Then there was the matter of tents, and flags, and banners, and tables, and chairs, and a kitchen, for the cooking of food. Her head started to spin at the thought of all these things to be done; it would take a week or more, at least.

Chapter 19

~ a bad Dream ~

Emerauld had yet to have her coronation, proclaiming her Queen. And the placing of the royal crown upon her head, thus, showing the faith the people had in her, that she would rule the kingdom, with a kind and gentle hand, fairly. She thought the coronation could be made to fit in quiet nicely, along with the festivities and banquet. It would be an excellent time for it, since everyone would be gathered for the feast.

The religious clergy would performed the coronation, and bestow their blessings on her, in sight of the vast throngs of people, who would be attending the celebration. It would be one grand event she envisioned, smiling.

~ ~ ~

She sent for the heads of the castle staff and when they had all gathered together in the great room, she told those that were in charge, what she desired. All their heads nodded in agreement, as their eyes followed her as she walked around the room speaking.

She proceeded to delegated duties, to those in charge, along with any other such things she could think of, that still needed doing. This in turn, was partially delegated to their underlings. Still, she worried about all the functions and when it would take place.

Scurrying about without making a protest, people were doing what was expected of them, getting everything in place.

She worried still, if everything could be accomplished on time. She was sure, some of the pain in her head, was partially due to the hurrying to get everything ready on time. She tried to ignore it. Maybe it would go away.

Two days later, Emerauld awoke in a cold sweat, her head tight with fear of an impending disaster. She had had a vivid dream that frightened and woke her sometime before daybreak. The dream had been confusing. It was erratic, all mixed up. She had to tell someone.

Her first thought was Alaric. She could ask his advice. She thought back to when he had first entered the cave chamber, where she was held prisoner, she had been drawn to him instantly. Later she had fallen in love with him and there was no one else she could turn to. She decided on telling Alaric of the dream.

It was like a premonition of events to come. Some of the dream had been frightening, leaving her feeling apprehensive and cold, but other parts had been wonderful, leaving her with a warm feeling. She made up her mind to discuss it with him at the morning meal. They could decide then what to do about the dream, if anything.

She dressed simply, and then walked down the stairs and through a short hallway, into the dining room. It was empty except for one lone figure, sitting at the long oak table. Her heart leapt, it was Alaric.

He was taking a drink from his mug. He saw her and stood as she approach, and held a chair for her. He said, "Emerauld you're up very early." He looked at her pale white face which held a furrowed frown. "Something's wrong?" Taking her hand in his, he said, "Tell me."

"I'm worried about my sister. I had such a terrible *dream* last night. Well not all of it was bad. There were good parts too." She brushed the hair back from her face. "Oh Alaric, I'm so glad I have you. You don't know how much I love you." He started to talk, but she pressed two fingers on his lips stopping him. "But I love my sister too."

"I know." He said, squeezing her hand.

"Alaric, I must tell you about my dream." She paused, took a deep breath, trembled slightly, and began. "It's jumbled up in my head, so bear with me and hear me out. First, remember when I told you about the time my sister, Gur, and I, went exploring into a cave with a long tunnel, which split apart into two tunnels. Gur took one tunnel and I took the other, remember? Then with my meeting the Lady in White, down the tunnel I took. I don't know what happened to Gur in the tunnel she chose, but when she came out, she was changed, somehow."

"The Lady in White came to me in my dream last night. With a warning, my sister is going to escape from the castle. She said my sister would try to go back to the tunnel where she was changed. She said I must stop her. I must not let that happen. If she goes into that tunnel, she will be changed forever. All hope for her then would vanish."

"She said there was a chance of changing my sister back to the sister I knew, when we were young. I was told, I must stop her from going into the tunnel where she was changed. It is evil."

"I must stop my sister, The Lady in White said. I should take her instead, into the tunnel where she resides, the one I had taken. I must bring my sister to her. She said it might be the last chance, to change my sister back as she was before. And if my sister escapes from the castle, and is caught by the people, they will surely hang her. That is all I remember of the vision."

"You've told me about the warnings." Alaric said. So, tell me now, what was the good part of your dream?"

She shook her head, looked down and murmured. "I dreamed that we would be wed after the coronation."

"Oh, great, then will I be King?" He asked, kissing her on the forehead.

"And there is more. Your brother is in love with Miiliinda, and I am sure she returns that love. We could maybe have them get married at the same time. What do you think? It would be one great extravaganza, which would not soon be forgotten. It would be talked about, around the country for years."

"It sounds like you have it planned to perfection. First, though, I think we should take your sister to this cave you speak of where she was changed. We must do it before she has any chance to escape. Then we shall see if Lady in White really can work a miracle."

Suddenly through the open dining room door, a guardsman, out of breath rushed up. He bowed, "Your Majesty, Gurgold has escaped. I came as fast as possible to tell you, The two guards, who were watching her, were found lying on the floor in front of the open doorway to her room. They both had a large bloody knot on the back of their head. We searched the room, but she was nowhere to be found, so I came here forthwith." He bowed again and stood at attention awaiting her orders.

Stunned at this news, Emerauld's hand flew involuntary to her mouth as she gasped. While the other hand clutched frantically at Alaric's arm. Her face pale, held a look of fear. She took one look at Alaric. "My dream has become reality."

"We must stop her from reaching that awful cave." She let go of his arm and turning to the guardsman said, "There is no time to loose, tell the Capitan of the guard to gather his men and meet us at the stables." The guard hurried off to do as instructed.

Emerauld a little unsteady from the news leaned against Alaric for support, but quickly overcoming her emotions she said. "We have no time to waste we must get to the stables and mount up."

By the time they got to the stables, even though they had rushed, Captain Jordaar and the Guardsmen were mounted and impatient to ride. It took very little time for Alaric and I to saddle up, we were ready.

Since, I was the only one who new where my sister was headed, I led the way and the rest followed behind in columns of threes, Alaric rode by my side. He said, "You think she is headed for the cave. What if you're wrong and we don't find her, what then?"

"You forgot my vision in the dream. She will go there as long as there is a breath left in her body. Something evil draws her to that place. Somehow it controls her; it will never let her go." She kicked her stallion, and increased its speed to a fast gallop.

Chapter 20

~ *transformation* ~

The countryside soon turned into rolling hills dotted here and there by larger hills. To me it felt similar to Emerauld's description. A short time later we came to the river called Grazalor. The water was not swift. We urged our mounts into the flowing waters that reach up almost to our stirrups. We had no problems crossing, the river was not running full.

After crossing and riding up the far bank, everyone began to regroup. Standing as tall as I could in the saddle, I looked for the small mountain Emerauld had described in one of our talks. I didn't see it, but a movement in the distance caught my eye and held it. Far ahead, a lone rider rode across the dusty plains, still too far away to make out if it were a man or a woman.

Whoever it was, they were far ahead and a lot of ground separated us, and them. The shimmering air from the heat that rose from the hot sands, made it hard to judge distances. We would have to draw closer to the rider, before we could tell if it was Gurgold or not. Nevertheless, seeing a rider this far from the castle, made us spur our horses to an even faster pace.

We were gaining on the rider when a small rounded mountain came into view in the distance. To me, it looked to be the mountain Emerauld had described. We were getting closer to the rider, who we could now see was a woman. The rider still some distance ahead must have seen us, for suddenly her horse kicked up dust, as it raced toward the small round mountain.

The rider was halfway between us and the mountain. By the time we caught up with whoever it was, they would have reached the mountain. If we were to catch the rider, it was going to be close. I yelled, "Its Gurold, we must catch her before she gets to the cave, or all will be lost." We had to try. We spurred our horses even faster. The race was on, our lives depended on it.

We were within three hundred yards when Gurgold reached the foot of the hill, leapt from her horse, and was scrambling up the hill, like a mad woman. Emerauld, jumped from her mount and being lighter, and swifter, and more agile, than the rest said, "Everyone follow me, I know where she is going, she's headed for the cave."

No one talked as we climbed the hill. We dodged around boulders, and small shrubs, like ants whose nest has been disturbed. We spread apart in our pursuit. Some were faster at traversing the hillside than others. Breathing hard from exertion, we drew closer to our quarry. I could hear her grunts and other strange sounds, as she struggled in her climb, spewing forth from her vile, wicked mouth. It was nothing a child should hear. She was gasping for breath as we drew closer.

On the hillside directly ahead, beside a gigantic boulder, a cave opening came into view. Gurgold change course and headed straight for the dark opening. She would reach the cave before us, but not by much. Just a little more and she would be caught, I thought as she disappeared into the dark mouth of the cave.

The men started to give up. Emerauld shouted at them, "We cannot stop and quit when we are this close." Standing at the caves mouth facing the men, arms spread wide, she screamed out, rallying them to action. "The tunnel is very long and very dark. Therefore, it is hard to make much speed. So you see there is still time." She turned and disappeared into the dark opening. "We have not much time left so hurry men," Echoed from out of the darkness. Then very faintly came. "There is still time for us to stop her, before she reaches her destination."

Emerauld had vanished into the darkness, and directly behind her I followed. Shortly after came the Captain and Vaadar, then the rest surged in around me. Upon entering the cave, I was momentarily blinded. Until my eyes adapted to the darkness, I was not able to see a thing only the dim light that filtered in through the entrance from outside.

As I felt around in the dark, my hand touched the rough dirt wall of the cave. Slowly we progressed feeling our way along the tunnel, bumping each other, until our eyes adjusted somewhat to the dark.

Emerauld stopped and said, "We need some kind of a light. Did anyone bring a lantern?" No one had had the foresight to bring a lantern. Then she exclaimed, "Wait, something is happening to me, I have a strange tingling feeling." Then amazingly, Emerauld started to glow, a strange light emitting from her, casting enough light for us to see a few feet ahead into the dark. Being able to see, we moved rapidly along the tunnel.

"How far is it to where the tunnel splits?" I Ask.

Hesitantly, Emerauld's voice drifted back over her shoulder, as she hurried forward, "It's still some distance ahead, I think. I'm not sure just how far. I was only here once. But it makes no difference; the sooner we catch my sister the better we will be."

No more was said after that. Breathing hard from exertion the rest of us, trying not to be trampled, rushed forward trying to keep up with the glowing Emerauld, who miraculously seem to almost float, she moved so rapidly along. Suddenly it seemed warmer and hotter, and I became aware of an increasingly foul odor. The heat, combined with the dampness, brought a smell of mustiness to my nose. It smelled like something had died a long time ago. Ignoring the smell, I tried to keep up.

Rounding the bend as the tunnel turned sharply left, we saw Gurold. Mumbling incoherently, she stumbled and fell. Before she could regain her feet, Emerauld said, "Captain Jordaar, please bind her hands so she cannot free herself. I've had enough of this escapade."

Captain Jordaar did as ordered, and then holding firmly to Gurgold, turned and started back toward the entrance but was stopped by Emerauld. "Wait." She said. "Alaric, you remember my dream?"

"Yes, I remember. The dream was about the three of us, your sister, yourself and me."

"Remember the vision I had? I was supposed to take my sister into the tunnel, the one which I had taken. Remember?

"Yes what about it?"

"It makes no sense in taking her back to the castle, when we are only steps away from where I was told to take her. Don't you agree?"

She was right of course. So I said, "You are so right in your thinking. So lead the way."

Emerauld gave orders to Jordaar that under dire consequence, no one would be allowed to follow us deeper into the tunnel. And no one was to be allowed to leave, either.

I held Gurold by an arm, Emerauld grasped the other and we walked off into the dark tunnel. Emerauld still glowing led the way. The others were left standing in the dark as we moved further along. We rounded another bend and I could see a faint glow ahead which grew brighter and brighter as we drew closer. It became so bright that I clinched my eyes tight, leaving only a slit to see from. Then the light swirled around us for a moment, and then came a voice, heard in my head and not with my ears. It was soft and compelling, melodic and hypnotizing.

The voice said, "Welcome Emerauld my sweet child. The vision sent you, must have worked! Good. May I presume... this ugly creature to be your sister? The one infected with evil. So full of the wickedness she is filled, it makes her puffy and fat. This one I shall purge of all her dark powers, and evil thoughts, and return a sweet loving sister to you."

Being slightly nervous, I began shaking. The light swirled around me, calming me and the voice spoke. "Alaric, be not afraid no harm shall come to you."

After calming Alaric, the voice continued, "So... this is your sister." The brightness swelled in intensity, and swirled about us, with the fury of a tornado. The last I saw of Emerauld and her sister Gurgold, they were swept up, taken from the floor they disappeared into the swirling, blinding, white light.

It became quiet; I thought I had lost my hearing. Suddenly an ear-screeching scream pierced my head. The screams were enough to curdle ones blood and freeze their heart. The swirling light gradually changed from white to black, then to blue, then to green and then finally back to white. The screams and screeching grew so loud that I clasped both hands over my ears. I could still hear them, even though my hands covered my ears. The screams suddenly stopped as fast as they had started. A slight smell of rotten eggs and burnt sulfur lingered in the air for a moment.

It was dead silent. I thought for a moment I had lost my hearing, it was so quiet. I opened my eyes to the sound of joyous laughter. Only remnants of white light still swirled softly around the two sisters, who stood in its midst embracing.

"Alaric, this is my true sister. Gur say hello to the man who is soon to be my husband."

To my utter amazement, Gurold was no longer fat and ugly. She had been transformed into a pleasantly, good-looking woman. She took a step toward me and I backed away a step. "Alaric, you no longer have reason to fear her, she has been wholly cleansed. All the evil has been driven from her." Emerauld laughed. Then the three of us laughed. But I was still not sure.

We found our way back along the tunnel, to the others, and on out onto the hillside, and the fresh, wonderful air. Out in the sunlight, those who had come in contact with Gurgold before, were truly amazed, they marveled at the apparent transformation.

Arriving back in the city, the news of Gurgold's cleansing of her evil spirit, and the complete transformation of herself, spread quickly throughout the kingdom. And following close upon that revelation, came the announcement of Emerauld's coronation and the ritual of crowning her Queen. To be followed immediately with her wedding.

A great party was planed and its preparation set into motion. Invitations were sent by the fastest couriers. Nobles far and wide were invited to attend this glories extravaganza to be held in a fortnight.

For all many guests which would be attending the coronation, the wedding, and a large feast which would follow, accommodations were made. Then too, there were the frivolities which would be sure to follow. There would most certainly be a few who would celebrate too much, having more wine than they should. They could become quite rowdy. Therefore, security was discussed in the course of one of the many meetings held.

"Captain Jordaar, you do understand what I expect from your men? I surely do not want a repeat like the last one, where my sister took the throne, and most guests were held captive."

"Your highness, I assure you, you need have no doubts. I have trained the Elite Guards for all contingences. I might add, with much more discipline. They are well trained and ready."

"Good. I have watched the training and I do believe, there are few that can stand up to them. You have done well Captain, you're to be commended." He started to leave but was stopped in midstride, "Oh, Captain! There is one question that I must ask. I am curious about something."

She smiled, showing a flash of white teeth. "Do you ever miss being a Raven?" She asked.

The Captain returned her smile, "Sometimes, I do miss winging it high in the sky, way up above the clouds, and looking down at all that lies below." There was a tinge of a caw in his voice as he choked slightly. Then he laughed and she joined in.

Chapter 21

~ the Coronation ~ the Crown ~

Emerauld was caught up in the planning, along with her sister Gurgold, and together they burned many a candle, late into the night, planning all the details. She had more help than she needed, along with too many suggestions from her newly made friends who had participated in saving her from the Crystal Cave.

There was so much to do and so little time to get it accomplish. Someone mentioned food and another joined in. "Yes, we mustn't forget, there will be hundreds of hungry people to feed. We will have to gather together a working food preparing group."

We ended up with 10 kitchen cooks, and selected one, to be the head chef, and to oversee the rest. He in turn hired 20 assistants, to help in the preparation of food. After which he hired 15 servers, both men and women, to carry out the steaming food, which would be piled high on trays, and served on the extra large, 25-foot long wooden tables. The tables were to be placed randomly about on the gentle rolling green hillside directly down the hill from the castle entrance.

Seamstress, Tailors and Clothiers with their many bolts of colorful cloth fabric were sent for. They would be needed to create divine gowns, for the ladies, and handsome attire for the men. Then too, tents of all colors were needed, for varies uses. Therefore, tent makers were included in the group. Boot and shoemakers, almost as an after thought, were also sent for.

To make sure the apparel would fit properly, several measurements, and fittings, were required by the tailors, and the seamstress. The last of the garments were completed and ready with just two days time remaining, before the blessed event.

~ ~ ~

Soon the outlying nobles started arriving, most rode in splendid carriages, with lots of finery that sparkled, from spit and polish, accompanied by their footmen. Others arrived on horseback, and some came in plain unadorned horse-drawn carts and some came on foot. The lawns began to swell with the many people of every kind, size and occupation.

Children were screaming, and running, and playing with balls. Adults stood talking in small groups watching, the comings and goings of noblemen and women, farmers, soldiers, sheepherders, shopkeepers and the multitude of people. The festivities had started early, before it was announced.

It was mid morning; a cool gentle breeze flowed around the colorful tents. Long narrow banners, fluttered from tent tops. Bright red and blue flags displaying the royal crest in gold, waved restlessly, as they hung from the castles turrets. Horses snorted, mothers yelled at their rambunctious offspring. Citizens, some with mugs of ale, and some holding a glass filled with wine. Everyone seemed to be enjoying a fun day.

The chef's had been overly busy for a week, in the cooking and preparing of food. As an afterthought, wine merchants were called upon to supply the dark red liquid. After all the hard work, now at last, it was all coming together, finally.

Colorful tents dotted the landscape, punctuated here and there with the long wood tables, which sat haphazardly about. Meandering crowds of people wandered past the tents, stopping now and then to gawk, at the merchants hawking their wares. The merchants were never one to miss a chance for profit. Everyone was thinking big.

It was mayhem, loud and noisy. A raucous group of young ladies bantered back and forth to one another, yelling they flirted with a group of young men, some of dubious character. Others, as they met old friends, hugging and patting of backs. Men, kissing women they did not know, and some of the woman, responding by returning the kiss. Some groping here and there followed sometimes. Everyone was having a grand, merry time. Not everyday did one get to attend a royal coronation, followed by a wedding, all on the same day.

Around midday, the castle doors swung wide, and out marched eight trumpeters, dressed in crimson coats and adorned with brass buttons, and wearing dark blue pants with a crimson stripe running down each leg. No one took notice of the eight as they marched quickly, to a small knoll, which rose slightly above the tents and the milling citizens.

They split into rows of two, four to a side, and taking five steps apart turned and faced towards the center, forming a corridor directly in front of the open castle doors. The Master Trumpeter spoke, and they snapped to attention. With a nod from the Master, they raised their trumpets to tight lips, and blew. The masses stopped, as every head quickly turned toward the attention getting fanfare.

Then Emerauld appeared in a gown of white, trimmed with gold. The trumpets blared again; Emerauld strode forth to stand before the crowd. With glistening eyes, she looked down upon those who would soon be her subjects. The Elite Guardsmen stood to one side, discreetly alert. An entourage of several friends stood a small distance behind, including Alaric at the forefront, along with Tagg, who was smiling ear to ear.

All was quite as she spoke. "My dear citizens, people from the surrounding outer regions, noblemen and women, and humble peasants," She spread her arms wide, taking in the upturned faces of the many. "I bid you welcome, one and all, on this joyous occasion to witness and to celebrate with me, my coronation as your Queen. I plan on making many changes to our laws and taxes. They will be changed to be fairer to those of you that have so long struggled to pay Queen Gurgold her taxes, and tried in vain to obey her laws. I will govern and rein benignly. If there are any disputes or quarrels between your selves, it shall be settled fairly, as will be any disagreements with me."

She paused, taking a deep breath, and said, "You have all been invited here to witness this momentous event my Coronation and the Crowning. And I wish for all, to enjoy the festivities of this grand event. Now it is time." Cheers rang out across the hillside.

Emerauld signaled with a wave of her hand and four large men emerged from the castle carrying a huge, ornately carved wooden chair. Solemnly they placed the chair carefully upon the grass. Making sure it was stable; they stepped away, joining with the other observers. This would take the place of the throne in absents.

Out from the castle came three solemn faced clergymen, each dressed in a long black robe, followed yet by another, wearing a brown robe. The last carefully stepped forward, hands clenched tightly to a small blue pillow, upon which rested a beautiful crown of gold, set with radiate gemstones.

The three black robed men stopped in front of Emerauld. One spoke. "My Lady Emerauld, this is truly a glories' day for the kingdom of Fen-Millar." He then turned and spoke to the hundreds of people that stood silent, watching the ceremony in awe, having never seen a Coronation before.

With a voice both loud and deep, it carried across the vale, reaching to most that had gathered for this momentous occasion. "My fellow citizens and honored noble guest, this is a great moment for rejoicing, and celebrating."

The crowd didn't want a long speech and yelled for him to hurry up, and get on with it. "As you well know being first-born, Emerauld has first right to the throne, not Gurgold. Therefore, Emerauld is the rightful heir to the throne. Now that time has come."

Standing one to each side of Emerauld, two of the blacked robed clergymen gently grasped an elbow and escorted her to the wood throne. She was seated. Placing her arms on the armrest, she smiled and waited.

The head clergy said a few more words, and then he gave the clergyman holding the crown a nod. He quickly stepped forward to stand beside the throne. Emerauld's eyes darted to the crown and her smile grew larger. The head clergy took the crown from the pillow. Holding it in front of Emerauld, he uttered several words, which no one understood, Then he placed the crown on Emerauld's head and said in a loud ringing clear voice, "I crown you, Queen Emerauld."

Responding to the crowning of Emerauld, the people began cheering, others applauded and some yelled, and screamed loudly, for several minutes

Emerauld looked serious for a moment, adjusted the crown to her liking, then arose from the chair and facing her subjects, quieted their fervor and said, "To all who are gathered here I thank you. It is a great privilege and an honor to serve you, as did my father before me." A tear trickled down her cheek. "I will be a true and just queen to all." She paused wiping away the tear with a fingertip and smiled.

She held out her arms and said. "Let the celebration begin." Her words were greeted with more cheers and yells, followed by shouts of, "Live long Queen Emerauld." She stood waving and smiling for a time. Alaric came to her side, and with a grin gave a slight bow, "My Queen." Then he looked around making sure no one else could hear and said in a whisper, "The Queen, I completely adore and love."

Tagg who was never far away rushed up and not one to be outdone, he stepped forward smiling, and also bowed, his eyes bright, he said, "My Queen too." Together, arm in arm, the three went up the steps into the castle.

Chapter 22

~ two Weddings ~

Once inside, Emerauld grabbed Alaric, and bestowed a passionate kiss on his lips. He didn't resist, after all, she was the Queen. They embraced until Tagg tugged at her gown and whispered, "The head clergy is coming."

"My Lady, the nobles and ladies along with your few invited guest await you in the chapel. I am afraid they are growing impatient. Everything is ready as you have planned. Only your presence, and that of this handsome young man at your side, is all that is required." The clergyman turned and led the way.

"What is this you have planned, without telling me?" Alaric asked, "And just why do they await us in the chapel?"

"It's a surprise I have planned for you, my love." She smiled, grabbed him by the arm and pulled him along, hurrying after the clergyman. "Be patient, you will see soon enough."

Turning left from the main corridor, they stepped into the chapel. All Fifty or so invited guest stood, as the Queen entered. She led Alaric by his hand straight down the aisle as he gazed about in complete bewilderment. To each side sat rows of straight-backed wooden bench-seats. All those standing had their eyes focused on the Queen and the man with her. The clergyman stood waiting beside a dais.

The clergyman gave a sign for all to be seated. Still in a daze, Alaric faced Emerauld. She held his hands tightly with hers as if he might escape.

The clergyman read for a few minutes from a large book placed on the dais. Finished with the reading he raised a hand and blessing them pronounced them wedded.

It all had happened so fast. Alaric was not sure what had taken place until Emerauld held him close and whispered in his ear, "Kiss me my husband." The observers applauded as the newlyweds kissed. "Everyone, I would like to introduce you to my husband, and King of Fen-Milar."

"Here, Here," echoed wall to wall as best wishes were given. One of the nobles, a count, or baron, or something approached and congratulated the newly wedded Queen and a somewhat dismayed 'King Alaric.' With a guttural accent, he said, "It is not often, that one attends a Coronation of a Queen, and then her wedding, all on the same day. It is a most wondrous and unusual thing, you surely must be blessed."

Emerauld held up a hand and said, "All here are welcome to attend my wedding feast that will be held in the great hall." She led the way still holding on to the new groom. As she hurried along, she turned her head, and called happily over her shoulder, "Let us all celebrate this glorious moment."

Food and drink had already been placed on the tables at one end of the great hall, awaiting only the guest. At the other end sat several musicians, playing, a slow waltz of sorts. Between the food at one end and the music at other, the room had been cleared. Bare of its furnishings the polished stone floor was ready to be danced upon.

A duke, from another country, commented to his companion that the waltz was nice, but somewhat slow for his taste. Maybe something a bit faster, he suggested, would suite him fine. Emerauld overhearing the Dukes remark turned to him saying, "One of our court musicians has composed a new kind of melody. And another has figured out simple dance steps to fit the music. They call the music and steps 'The Chambilina.' It is a somewhat faster piece though, so it may be more to your liking,"

By the time she had finished talking to the Duke she had gathered a goodly number of people about her, who upon hearing her words, clamored to know more about this dance, called the Chambilina.

"Alright, I will explain the best I can on how to maneuver the steps, and to follow the cue of the rhythm. The Chambilina is a dance, somewhere between a waltz and marching music. The gentlemen are to twirl the ladies around and around to the music, like a waltz, only faster. The melody would then change, and the gentlemen would stop, separate from their partner, bow, and taking her hand march around their partner in time to the music, while she would turn in time to her marching partner, making one full circle the music would changed once more. Where upon the gentlemen would again hold their partners and waltz, spinning them graceful around."

Soon everyone was laughing at one another's mistakes. But a short time after and finally catching on, all were having a great time. Most all had pretty much got it after a few false starts. It was quiet a sight to see.

The ladies wearing elaborate gowns were held on the arms of the smiling gentlemen, dressed in gleaming uniforms. The ladies were spun around and around, their full-skirted gowns flaring as everyone spun, in unison, and in step with the music.

It was a grand sight to watch as all turned with a military precision, to the music, moving in and out and around. A grand sight, indeed.

The music stopped. Most of those dancing hurried to refill their glasses and a few nibbled at the food, while others paused to rest and catch their breath. They waited for the musicians to resume.

With this pause in the celebration, Emerauld got everyone's attention and said. "My dear friends I have many things I must attend to tomorrow, so I bid you all good evening." Every person stood and applauded her. She held up a long graceful hand and silence ensued. "But there is no reason for any of you not to continue on as long as you are able."

The Queen led Alaric to a tower far from all the noise and up the stairway to a large comfortable room. It was decorated to suite a woman. Oil lamps were dimly glowing casting flickering shadows. The Queen said, "Come my King consort it is time for our bed."

~ ~ ~

Seven days later, most of the royalty had left. The townsfolk, the farmers, the hired workers, were all back to their regular work. Some with aching heads. Most all were happy with the new Queen, except for one.

Raddick was happy on the one hand, but on the other, he was not really unhappy. His circumstances were troubling. He was envious of his brother becoming the King consort, and being so happy. While he, was stuck in quagmire.

He and Miiliinda had feelings for one another, and wished to be wed also. He hoped then they would be as happy as Emerauld and Alaric seemed to be. After stewing and mulling it over for several days, he worked up the courage, at Miiliinda's urging, to ask the Queen for permission for them to marry.

Raddick found Alaric and Emerauld, strolling hand in hand, along a stone path of the castles inner courtyard. The path curve gracefully in and out around flowering shrubs, which had been planted in the courtyards center surrounded by trees at the outer edges. It was beautiful, and quiet. Only the sound of doves cooing pierced its peaceful quietness.

"Raddick, how nice to see you this fine morning, it's been a few days. And, where is that beautiful girl Miiliinda? Ever since the spell which turned you into a wolf was lifted, you two have become inseparable."

Shyly he looked down and kicked at the stone paver. Then he looked up squarely at Emerauld and spoke, a slight quaver in his voice. "Your Majest... I... I mean... My Queen..." Then he blurted out, "I want to wed Miiliinda, and she wants to wed me. We love each other. So may we have your blessing and your help?"

Emerauld laughed at his halting speech and his frustration. "Oh, I'm truly sorry, I didn't mean to laugh, but... Yes, of course Raddick, you have my permission to wed Miiliinda. I will arrange it. Now hurry, go and tell her the good news."

"Thank you, my Queen." He started to leave, stopped and said, "Hello, brother. You can come to my wedding if it's alright with the Queen and she gives you permission" Laughing and in good spirits, he hurried off to tell Miiliinda the good news.

And so they were wed. The ceremony was not a long drawn out affair as was Emerauld's. Along with a few others, Gurgold attended, as did Vaadar and Captain Jordaar. It was a small gathering, held in.; the chapel, and preformed by the head clergyman.

Afterwards, in a small alcove off of the chapel, all those in attendance raised a glass of wine in a toast to Raddick and Miiliinda, for a long life, blessed with many children. Individually they stepped forward, hugging and slapping Raddick on the back, and in turn gently taking Miiliinda's offered hand and kissing it. Although the room was small, it was filled wall to wall with well-wishers, holding wine glasses as they mingled laughing and conversing with others.

"That was nice. It was short and sweet." Emerauld said giving Alaric a kiss on his cheek.

He kissed her on a cheek and said, "My love, now that my brother and his love are bound together as one, why don't we leave. I'm sure in this crowd we wouldn't be missed."

Emerauld quickly glanced about. With all the wine, they had consumed some of the well-wishers, especially the women, were not holding up to well. "Speaking of being missed, I don't see Gurold anywhere. Surely she's here. Do you see her?"

Alaric looked. "No, she's not here that I can see. She's gone."

Shortly after the ceremony, Gurgold with her head throbbing had slipped away. She had wandered off to be somewhere quiet. She had a need to listen to the voice which angrily echoed through her head.

Chapter 23

~ *lightning Bolts ~ a pink Cloud* ~

"Why is it that we so urgently need to find your sister? After all, we saved her from the evil that had control over her."

"Alaric, we must find her quickly before something catastrophic befalls us, all." She answered, anguish showing on her face. "In the past few nights, I have started having those dreams again, and the premonitions. I didn't tell you because I thought they were just dreams, but they have been growing, increasingly more urgent and real. I didn't say anything. I didn't want to worry you, but I have a feeling we must find her now!"

Without further adieu, Captain Jordaar was sought from amongst the many, mingling guest. They spotted him in a corner, trapped by two elder ladies, deep in conversation. People made way for the Queen and I followed behind.

Approaching the ladies she said, "Please excuse my intrusion, but I must speak with the Captain in private. It is most urgent." The ladies wondered off in search of a male that was unoccupied.

"Yes my Queen, what is it that is so urgent?"

"Have you seen Gurgold?"

Captain Jordaar glanced quickly over the room, his eyes missing nothing. "It appears she is no longer here. Do you wish for me to find her?"

"I fear the dark evil has reasserted itself upon her. She replied. If so, she must be found immediately before it can grow stronger. Have your men search the castle and grounds, forthwith."

"Yes your Majesty at once." He saluted smartly, spun on his heel and was gone.

"If Jordaar doesn't find her, she may try to make her way back to the evil dark cave, to regain her power. The Lady in White hoped that she had been purged of all evil, but some little remnant may still be lodged in her."

Alaric, striving to cheer her, said, "Do not worry my love, she may have just wondered off for some reason. Jordaar will find her, I'm sure.

But, Jordaar did not find her. An hour or more had passed when Jordaar reported back.

"Majesty, as instructed I had a hundred of the guardsmen search the castle and grounds. There is no sign of Gurgold."

"Captain, select your ten best guardsmen and meet Alaric and me at the stables. Go quickly now, there is no time to lose."

With her long legs, Emerauld holding her skirt high, rushed up the stairs, taking the steps two at a time. Dashed into her chambers and shedding her gown, dressed in ridding attire. By the time, we got to the stables our horses had already been saddled. Captain Jordaar and his hand picked guards were all mounted. Waiting and ready to ride. Emerauld led the way, her stallion being by far the fastest. Alaric and the guards followed not far behind.

After two hours of hard riding, we came to the river called Grazalor. Emerauld pointed at something crawling up the far riverbank. It was Gurgold, drenched and dripping muddy water from the river as she tried to crawl up the wet bank. She must have fallen from her horse or else it had thrown her. Either way we had her before she could reach the dark cave.

We rode our horses across and two of the guardsmen dismounted to help her, but she fought them. Biting, kicking, clawing and screaming at the top of her lungs in that language we could not understand, she was dragged the rest of the way up the slippery slope.

Emerauld jumped down from her stallion, and said, "Good work Captain." She walked to where Gurgold still struggled, to no avail, being held by two strong six-foot guardsmen. As Emerauld approached, she spat and uttered a string of foul sounding words. "Bind her wrist," was all

Emerauld said.

. While the three of us tried to decide what to do with Gurgold. The guardsmen that were not holding Gurgold led their horses along with ours, to the river to drink.

The Captain was for putting her into the castles dungeon. Alaric stood silent, thinking. Emerauld looked at them and said, "Well I can't keep my sister a prisoner untill I die, I just can't. There must be another way." While we thought about our quandary, a guardsman rode up having retrieved Gurgold's horse which had not wandered far off.

Emerauld suddenly brightened. I know what needs to be done. It was part of my dream. In all the confusion of the chase, I must have somehow forgotten it.

Emerauld said, "The Lady in White appeared to me in my dream. She told me if Gurgold ever tried for any reason, to go back to the cave, she must be stopped before entering it. And, if we caught her we should immediately take her to the place in the cave where we took her before. The Lady in White then said, there might still be time to save her, but we must hurry, she said time was important. The longer we wait the harder it is to bring her spirit back."

Alaric, running his fingers through his hair said. "What are we standing here for, then? Let us go." Quickly they rode to the foot of the dome shaped hill and just as quickly they dismounted. Alaric took notice that the group numbered fourteen. It was a good thing that there were fourteen he thought, *for thirteen was considered to be a bad omen.*

It took four guardsmen to half carry the still fighting and struggling Gurgold, as they struggled up the slope. At the caves entrance Emerauld selected four guardsmen to accompany us, along with the two which held the squirming Gurgold. We left the Captain and the remaining guardsmen, guarding the entrance and plunged into the black depths of the musty smelling tunnel.

Feeling our way, we had traveled only a short distance, when Emerauld's body began to glow dimly in the dark. The guardsmen who escorted the fighting, devil woman, gasped in surprised. Taking in a deep breath, they tightened their grip on Gurgold even tighter than before, expecting a trick or something. Emerauld herself was also surprised. Now with the faint glowing light that surrounded her, we found our way swiftly along the dimly lit tunnel. Soon we came to where the tunnel split apart. We took the right hand tunnel. The farther we progressed, the brighter the light became, that emanated from Emerauld.

It seemed we had not gone far, but when I looked back, the entrance was barely visible. Seeing a glimmer of light ahead in the distance, we hurried on and rounding a bend, we stopped. There suspended above the earthen floor was the *Lady in White*. She floated in the midst of a cloud of swirling white light, which surrounded her, with such brilliance, it was almost blinding.

A voice in my head said, "Welcome. I have been expecting you." The guardsmen nervously looked at one another. Emerauld seemed to be in another world. Gurgold, being in the presence of the great *Lady in White*, had stopped her struggling and stood not moving, dazed.

The white light swirled around Emerauld and Gurgold. Embracing then both, they disappeared into its white light. I had heard the ancient language coming from the *Lady in White* before. Now it bounced around in my head again. It sounded more like a recited chant or spell. Nevertheless, I did not understand one word of it.

The three had vanished into the swirling white light, which now appeared to be a white cloud, suspended between the caves floor and its ceiling. Gradually the white light faded to an evil looking black, and then slowly turned a dark brown, then to tan, then to a deep red, then to pink, then to green, then to yellow, and finally ending with a great blinding flash, it turned a brilliant white. The two guardsmen and I blinded for an instant, rubbed at our tearing eyes. Once our eyes returned to normal and we could see again. Emerauld and Gurgold standing together, gazed, happily at each other in wonder. The *Lady in White* stood, watching.

Some of the guardsmen began to regain their senses, having collapsed from the spectacle and the voice that echoed around inside their heads. It had been too much for the weak at heart. Overcoming their fright, they cautiously gathered around the two sisters. After a moment Emerauld spoke. "My sister has been returned to me and she is wholly cured. Let us all return to the castle and give thanks and celebrate."

The guardsmen gave out a disjointed, hearty yell of approval and we started retracing our path back to the entrance. Where I am sure, the Captain waited impatiently, wondering about the outcome, hoping for good news. The tunnel was bright as day as we followed after the three ladies. The *Lady in White* was escorting us out for some reason. Maybe she was fearful for us. Maybe she came along to protect us, from the evil that existed, in the other tunnel. The evil dark-side.

The Captain with a curious, but hopeful look greeted us as we emerged from the dark cave. "All went well I presume?"

"Perfectly." Emerauld and I answered.

He looked quickly in Gurgold's direction and his eye lingered a moment, wondering. Satisfied his eye moved on to the Lady in White. "And who is this brightly glowing creature that accompanies you?"

"Please Alaric, would you explain to the Captain? I am somewhat weakened from the whole ordeal." Emerauld said, holding onto her sister's hand, happily.

"Come Captain, I will try my best to explain." The captain and I walked along shoulder to shoulder as I spoke. I told him all that I had seen. It took me some time to explain it all, as Captain Jordaar kept interrupting, with his questions.

The Captain and I led the way down the hill with Emerauld and Gurgold, walking arm in arm, laughing and chatting. The *Lady in White* glided close beside them, watching.

The hillside flattened into the meadow where we had left the horses tethered. They were contentedly, grazing on the tall grass. Upon reaching the horses, we all stood for a moment staring back at the rounded hill, an evil place. We started to mount.

Suddenly everyone stopped. With looks of bewilderment, they listened, to the voice in their heads. The voice echoed, "This place is evil and must be destroyed before it can do irreparable harm." All eyes turned to the *Lady in White*, for it was she that spoke.

We watched spellbound as she held her arms skyward. And speaking in the ancient language the sky which had been bright and clear began to darken. Then more ancient words fell from her lips, she wroth-forth a storm, with dark forbidding thunderclouds, which concealed the brightness of angry flashing lighting. The muffled booming thunder rolling inside the black cloud soon became earsplitting as the cloud drew closer. It was as if the *Lady in White* was a magnet, drawing the dark cloud to her.

The long deep rumbling of thunder surrounded us. Reverberating from the hillside it bounced back and forth, almost deafening, it was so loud. Flashing jagged streaks of bright lightening struck the earth close to us. The smell of ozone filled the air. The booming became extreme as the cloud seemed to move closer until it was directly above us.

The howling wind increased its intensity, we hardly could stand upright. Everyone cowered in fear, becoming deathly afraid. We clung to one another for support. Great bolts, of flashing lightning, struck the earth, with titanic force, followed swiftly by loud rolling claps of thunder. Many of the lightening bolts were directed toward the cave opening by the *Lady in White*. The following explosions were so forceful the hill trembled for a moment, boulders were blown apart, and falling dirt clods fell everywhere. It was devastating like the end of the world.

The *Lady in White* caught more lighting-bolts in her hands and flung several more towards the dark cave opening. As more bolts struck the hill, chunks' of dirt and rock were blasted far up into the air, and falling back most of the hill was gone now, only a pile of boulders, rocks and dirt remained. The hill was now of a somewhat smaller size. We stared at the white cloud swirling around the *Lady in White*. When the dust cleared, she was still with us, unharmed. Wonder of wonders, it was a miracle, she must have untold power.

She turned to Emerauld, "My child, I foresee, you will have a great life ahead, do not waste it. If ever you need me, I shall come. Do not forget me, think of me often. Now I must go." The white cloud swirled faster and faster around the Lady in white obscuring her from our sight. Then the small white cloud lifted up into the clearing sky, and there it drifted along with the other clouds. It was the only cloud to have a pink tinge. Surely, it must be only a reflection from the setting sun... or maybe, just maybe, a glowing happiness in the *Lady in White's* heart.

~ ~ ~

The small rounded mountain which had contain both evil and good, rumbled as tons of earth, boulders and rocks crashed filling the tunnel, then slowly settled more firmly into place, packing the earth tight over the tunnel.

There dwelled an Evil entity in the tunnel. The tunnel had collapsed from the many explosions, caused by lighting bolts, which the Lady in White had flung into it.

The evil that had been smothered still existed. Buried beneath tons of earth it was encased and trapped forever, in a tomb of dirt, rocks and boulders. It grumbled. Waiting... Someday... Someone would discover it... again.

~

Then far, far away, the bells in Chinnder started to ring....

CHAD'TU

A western novel

IN THE STYLE OF LOUIS L'AMOUR

Kelsie R. Gates

THIS NOVEL IS DEDICATED TO LINDA

Thhhhanks to the following people for their encouragement and support without whom I would still be struggling.
Tami Frias
Jack Morris
Don Coach
Warren Fenton

PROLOGUE

His name was Chad'tu, a name with a reputation. He was a white man, even though he had an Indian name. Chad'tu had a reputation that followed him, and sometimes even preceded him. A reputation that made men's blood run cold with fear. A man feared for the fastness of his guns and the deadly precision with which he used them.

He was a ruggedly handsome man, tall with dark skin and piercing black eyes of a devil. A mane of black hair touched his broad muscular shoulders, and sensuous lips that could on a moment twist from friendly, into a sardonic grin. He wore two Colt forty-four guns strapped around his narrow waist and tie to each leg. A man called Chad'tu by some, and to others he was just Chad, a fun loving man.

However, to one he was a loving husband.

CHAPTER 1

I rode down from the ridge of the Black Mountain range. Bone weary, I urged the horse down the rocky hillside. Covered with dust, I was dirty, thirsty and hungry. My horse, an offf-white appaloosa with scattered spots of rusty brown across her rump, was also tired. Faith was an amazing horse, tall and with the strength and spirit of fiiiive. I had raised her from the time she was a year old.

Head down, she slowly picked her way, slipping and sliding, down the steep rocky mountainside, headed toward home. It took all my strength to remain in the saddle as we descended the steep slope to the valley. I thought of the beautiful - red-haired woman with the mischievous deep green eyes that waited for me at the cabin. When I reached home, she would rush forth from the door throw her arms around me, and smother me in kisses.

* * *

I'd gone to the Black Mountains looking for a place to settle and raise cattle and maybe a son or daughter or both with God's blessing. Not fiiiiinding a suitable place after passing over a lot of country, I had fiiiiiinally settled on a grassy mesa edged high up against the granite side of Black Mountain. At fiiiiiirst sight, I knew this was the place to build and start my ranch and raise a family. Far from the towns that held the corruption of gamblers and drunken cowboys. Yes, this was the place to raise my family.

From high atop the mountain, a roaring waterfall tumbled several hundred feet down the shear granite rocks into a pond and then ran off into a creek and trickled on down the mountainside, slowly winding its way around aspens and sycamores. The creek finally ran off through the knee-deep grass. Signs of deer, wild pig, and turkey, along with coyote and wolf tracks were evidence of an abundant wildlife.

It took some time to build the cabin on this high plateau, which overlooked the vast surrounding country. For the convenience of the water, I had built close to a spring in the mountainside that flowed from the ground and meandered like a snake slowly back and forth across the downward slope until it joined into the waterfall. The view from the ranch was more than a man could ask for. It was about twelve miles from a new town.

The small town was so new it still had no name. A rock strewn dirt street

7

ran through the town. Across from the hotel was the Overland Stage stop. Next door was a stable with an adjacent corral. Next to the stable was the blacksmith shop, owned by John Hurley. A huge man that probable weighed close to two fifty, with arms as large as his head and a belly that matched. Everyone called him "Big John." He was a man you would not want to mess with.

Everyone who lived in town called it, 'No Name.' What the town did have was a general mercantile store, owned and run by John and Sara Bartlett, both hard working and friendly people. A saloon with a newly painted white sign that read in rather large gaudy red letters 'Pair-a-Dice' owned by a large handsome woman by the name of Maybelle. Those that were acquainted with her called her Belle. The saloon had a long bar down one side and games of chance on the other. A stairway in the back led to rooms above, some to let and others ... girls for an evening of entertainment.

Thhhe sheriff f f's offffiiice sat on a slight curve the street took at the edge of town, where usually you would fi i ind the sheriffff, kicked back in his chair, his scuffffed boots resting against the railing of the porch, puffffiiing on a cigar with an overview of the street. Sheriffffff Jay Reardon was a gentle man but if he got riled, you'd better watch your step. Thhhhe people in town were mostly friendly with the exception of the few rowdies that occasionally would pass through on their way headed west.

***

During the summer in this part of the country, the climate was good and the weather was mild, with only a few hot days. Thhhhhe several thundershowers that usually occurred kept the grass growing so there was plenty of grass to graze cattle. Winters were mild, with slight snowfalls that seldom covered more than two feet, three where the wind had blown snowdrifts up against a sharp out jutting of stone or over a gully.

Today, there was a gentle summer breeze blowing through the canyon. I was up before dawn and out rounding up strays. With an open range, they sometimes wander up canyons for no apparent reason that I could tell.

After two years of hard work, with one bull and fiifty or so head of cattle, I figured I was doing okay. My cattle, some with newborn calves were increasing nicely. Trying to increase the herd I could not afford to let them wander far from the ranch, a mountain lion might get hungry. I'd tried my best to keep the few cattle I had in one spot. With no fences, it was a full time job. It was worth the effort because of the beautiful woman, who supported my efforts, my wife who loved and adored me.

Rounding up loose cattle and leaving them with the herd, I'd headed for the cabin. Thoughts of my woman with long flaming red hair, which cascaded like a beautiful waterfall down past her shoulders, drifted into my head. A woman with a touch of the Irish spirit, as wild as she was beautiful.

With one hand, I pushed my hat back and wiped the sweat from my forehead and neck with a red bandanna. It was hot and muggy. I rode along thinking of Jaydeen. The shadows were growing long as the sun slowly slipped

8

behind Black Mountain. The temperature started to cool somewhat. I couldn't wait to get to the ranch and wrap her in my arms.

With that thought and a cooling breeze, I urged Faith on. Faith knew we were close to home and eagerly picked up the pace, ears forward and alert in anticipation of the wolf that usually bound out to greet us.

Approaching the ranch, I looked for the wolf called Track, which I and Jaydeen had nursed back to health. He had grown into a magnificent beast, which had bonded to both me and Jaydeen, like a brother. With pleasant thoughts, I remembered the day I had found Track.

* * *

I'd been out rounding up strays, when I heard the most pitiful cries of an animal. It sounded more like a whimper. Searching for the source, I found a small wolf cub in a small indentation in the side of a short bluff.

It looked like the bluffff had collapsed from a recent thunderstorm, bringing down brush and dirt, partially covering the small hole that concealed a pitiful starving wolf pup. It appeared to have been abandoned by its mother. For what reason I didn't know, maybe she couldn't get to it, and left it to die. Nevertheless, I took a sharp look around making sure the mother was not nearby.

A snarling vicious skinny ball of fur had greeted me as I pulled brush from the opening. Seeing a man, the pup tried to hide, but was too weak. Even though it was small, it snarled, trying to bite with its small razor sharp teeth. Taking no chances, I wrapped the snarling, biting, and kicking, wolf cub into my bedroll, gathered it up and taken it home.

'Track,' I had named the wolf ... usual ran out to greet me.

As I approached the cabin, I noticed there was no smoke coming from the chimney. Strange I thought it was unlike Jaydeen not to having a fiiiiiire going this time of day. Thhhhhhhe sun was almost beyond the horizon. It was starting to chill a little.

I rode up to the house wondering why Track had not greeted me. Dismounting I tied my horse to the hitching rail. I looked around wondering, and then stepped up onto the porch, walked to the door that stood slightly ajar and pushed it open and stepped inside.

Quickly I looked around and called her name. "Jaydeen ... Honey where are you?" She didn't answer. Then I noticed the broken dish on the floor and the overturned chair lying next to a red smear of blood on the stone floor. Worried, I called her name again. She did not answer.

I noticed a blood smear on the side of the doorway that I'd missed before. Was it her blood? Maybe someone or something had attacked her. I hoped it was not her blood. Something terrible must have happened. Concerned, I hurried to the barn she might be there. The stable was empty. Her horse was gone. She would never leave the ranch without telling me. A dark grey shape in the corner caught my eye. As I approached, the sound of a whimper cut the quiet.

9

Bending, I found my wolf beaten but still alive. Stroking and speaking softly, I soothed Track, running my hands over him feeling for broken bones or flesh wounds. There was none, only a patch of sticky fur. After some effort and with my help I got Track to stand. "What happened boy?" I said, stroking him gently. Standing with some effort, Track leaned against me, licked my hand, and feebly wagged his tail. I'd noticed Track had dried blood around his mouth. He must have gotten a good bite of someone. I said, "You'll be okay, seems like you got kicked, and ..." my voice trailing off I thought of Jaydeen and stepped out of the stall.

I checked the ground in front of the stable. Along with Jaydeen's there were three sets of boot prints in the soft earth. I bent and memorized them; I noticed one print was slightly drug through the dirt. It looked like Track did get a piece of someone. Mixed in among the boot prints were the fresh hoof prints made by three horses, hoof prints I did not recognize. I studied them so as not to forget them.

Becoming very worried, I went back to the house, with Track limping after. I tried to visualize what the hell had happened.

She must have struggled and put up one hell of a good fiiiight from the looks of the kitchen. Still, someone had taken her. She would never leave the ranch voluntarily. Why had they taken her? Was it her blood on the fllloor or that of her attackers? For what reason had they taken her? I didn't know. Thhhhhere were many questions, for which I didn't have answers.

I only knew what would happen when I caught up with them, and I would catch up with them. I vowed. As surely as the sun rises and sets, I would catch them. Thhhhhhey had no idea who they were dealing with. When I caught up to them ... what would I do ... Kill Thhhhem?

Getting a bucket of oats, I fed Faith. Going into the house, I hurriedly stufffffffed supplies into my saddlebag. I checked my Colt guns that I wore tied down. When I caught the men that had taken Jaydeen, I would kill them one and all. Grabbing the Winchester from the gun rack along with more ammunition for the riflllle and guns, I went outside.

Faith had fiinished eating and I led her over to the water tank to drink her fiill. With her nose to the water drinking, she seemed to sense my unease. I suddenly remembered the supplies went back into the house picked up the saddlebag that held food for a week or two, which ought to be enough. Faith had drunk her fill when I returned and was pawing the ground as if to say lets go.

Shoving the Winchester into the boot, I turned and quickly filled up two canteens I'd snagged hanging from a hook beside the door. I lashed down the saddlebag and bedroll and looping the straps of the canteens across the saddle horn, grabbed the saddle horn and jumping up, slid my boot into the stirrup and with one smooth motion, flipped the other leg over and stuck my boot into the stirrup.

The sun set low and was dropping rapidly to merge with the horizon. I gathered up the reins, took a long last look around before starting to track the four sets of hoof prints. If I were to catch them before dark, I'd not have much time. I looked back over my shoulder one last time as I urged Faith forward out of the yard at a fast trot.

The wolf limping slightly had started after me not wanting to be left behind. I quickly pulled up the horse and in a commanding voice said, "Stay. Track Stay ... Stay," I said to the wolf as I turned Faith and again headed out of the yard.

Track lay down and watched his master ride away. As soon as Chad and Faith were out of sight, he arose to follow. Track had a mind of his own and followed after them, limping slightly with his head down smelling the scent.

The anger and vengeance that burned hot and heavy in my heart spurred me on. My anger grew more with every breath. I had renewed energy, with but a single purpose, find and punish those responsible.

Faith sensing my mood started down the sloping hillside at a fast pace without urging, her head up and ears forward and alert. Thhhe sun dipped lower into the horizon, the sky turned grey and the shadows grew longer by the minute. Don't think just hurry and catch up, was the only thought on my mind. I started to lose hope as the shadows turned from grey to black and the sun quickly set beyond Black Mountain. I could not follow their trail in the dark.

Stopping Faith, I stood as tall as possible in the stirrups looking and smelling for a sign of smoke or the light from a campfiiiiire. Surely, they could not be more than four or fiiiive hours ahead. If so, I might see their campfiiiire. All I saw was the black of night.

Riding over to a grove of Sycamore trees that grew close by, I dismounted and tied my horse to a low branch. Somewhere offfffff in the dark a night owl hooted. I hastily started to climb the tree with the thought if I could get high enough I could see farther and spot their fiiiiire. Fifty feet up the tree, I stopped and catching my breath, looked hopefully out into the darkness. Nothing, no glow in the night sky, just the black of night sprinkled with a few stars. Then a wolf howled close by.

Smiling to myself, I slowly and carefully made my way down the tree. Waiting at the bottom was Track. If wolves could smile then he was smiling and happy to be with me.

Well one thing was for darn sure; I couldn't follow their trail in the dark. Searching about I gather some small dried out mesquite and dead branches from the sycamore and built a small sheltered fire in a gully that couldn't be seen if anyone looked this way. I put on my worn buckskin coat as the chill of the night started to creep in.

I filled the coffee pot with water and makings for coffee, setting it on rocks next to the fire to heat. While the coffee was making, I took the saddle off of Faith, setting it well back in the shadows of the trees away from the fire where I would sleep and not be a target. No one would surprise me. I grabbed a couple handfuls of dried grass and gave Faith a good rub down.

Track lay close to the fire, rested his head on his paws, his eyes reflecting the dancing flames he watched every move I made.

Pouring a cup of coffee, I sat on the ground next to my loyal wolf. "You and me, we'll get her back." At the sound of my voice, Tracks ears perked up and he thumped his tail. I gave him a pat and a piece of jerky I'd taken from the saddlebags. I chewed on my piece and Track on his.

Being tired, I rolled out my bedroll by the saddle, placed the Winchester's barrel on the saddle close at hand if needed and banked the fire. I lay down back in the shadows, a man could not be too careful in this country. If a man was not right careful, he could wake up dead. Shot or with an arrow sticking from his chest. I looked up at the stars through the branches, what would to-morrow bring? Track moved over and lay next to me. Throwing an arm over him, I soon fell into a fitful sleep.

I was up before the first light of dawn. Track had disappeared into the trees sometime during the dark morning hours. The wolf's leg had seemed **much better. I stoked up the fiire and cooked breakfast, bacon and red eye gravy along with cofffee. While eating, I watched for Track.**

I poured a second cup of coffffee. Track appeared as silent as a ghost from the edge of the trees, carrying in his mouth the bloody remains of a half-eaten rabbit. He approached the fi i i ire, dropped the rabbit at my feet, then lay down and fiiiinished the rest, fur, bones, and all. When he fiiiinished he licked his lips and looked up at me as if to say, my breakfast was better than yours.

In the cold morning hours before the fiiiirst light peaked over the horizon. I kicked dirt on the dying embers of what remained of the fiiiiire, making sure it was out, turned up the collar of my coat and buttoned it, and packed up the gear.

I was ready to mount Faith when I had a sudden impulse. Flipping the leather thong from the hammer of my Colt that held it secure in its holster, I pulled the gun in one smooth fast motion pointing it toward the horizon and fanned close to the hammer, with my left hand, while crouching making a noise like a kid when they shoot make believe guns.

Satisfiiiiiied with my draw ... I double checked the cartridges, replaced the Colt into the holster fastening the thong over the hammer to keep it in the holster if I had to ride hard. Satisfiied, I stepped into the leather and was on my way.

Track would lope along ahead and sometimes he would range out to the side with his head down smelling and sniffing. He ran as if his leg no longer bothered him. It appeared that he was almost fully recovered. Occasionally he would lift his head above the scrubby brush to make sure I was still in sight. He was a magnificent animal I loved dearly, but not as much as I loved Jaydeen.

I rode slowly till the sun peeked over the horizon, throwing enough light to see by. Finally, I picked up their hoof prints left in the dirt. Picking up their trail was easy and from the spacing of the hoof prints. It seemed they were taking their time wherever they were headed. Not knowing they were being pursued was all to my advantage.

I urged Faith into a slow gallop following the tracks in the direction the four horses and their riders had taken. With the dawning sun, sagebrush and yucca appeared from the plains. I urged Faith to a faster pace.

Trailing after them, the sun rose ever higher into a cloudless blue grey sky. I could tell it was going to be another hot day. Moving fast hour after hour, I tried to catch them. I couldn't tell if they were headed for the town called 'No Name.' Their trail looked to be angling off and heading past the town. I wondered where they might be headed.

A couple of times I lost the trail and started making wide swings and loops till I picked it up again. Why had they taken Jaydeen I kept wondering? There was no reason I could think of. I thought maybe it had to do with something that had happened in my past. I could have made a few enemies in the line of work I'd done in my younger days.

It got me thinking as I tracked the four riders relentlessly, hour after hour **in the blistering heat. I kept after the riders, who were somewhere still ahead. ... With the heat beating down my thoughts drifted back to the past ... back to every year of my past life that I could remember. I searched through my memories for an answer. What had I done in the past to deserve this?**